DAWN MATTER

A.J. CURRY

CROSSROADS OF CROSSTIME

VOLUME II

RCD PRESS
PORTLAND, OREGON
ROSECITY.DIGITAL

Table of Contents

Part 1: Breakfast at Epiphany's

one: murphy

The second fall was a lot worse—bad enough to get my attention.

After I got out of the hospital, I decided it was finally time to get real about this 'getting old' crap. I put everything in storage, put the house up for rent... and moved.

East Portland reminded me a lot of the neighborhood where I'd grown up and spent half my life: A place called 'Montrose,' in a city called 'Houston,' in a state called 'Texas'... that was more or less part of a country called 'America.' The names are all the same, but that's about it. I haven't aged gracefully. Neither has anything else in this world.

The housing co-op I bought into reminded me of my misspent youth even more than my new neighborhood. It had been a pretty common play back in the day to get together some friends and split the rent on an old, big house.

More often than not, it was my name on the lease. More often than not, I was the guy who made sure everyone was kicking in on the rent, and—more often than not—I was the guy who got to talk to the cops when the parties in those old houses got out of hand, got to explain to the occasional drug-dealing roommate the house rules, and got to explain to people who didn't understand the house rules that they were no longer welcome.

I never had a problem being 'the guy' or being the operative part of the phrase 'I know a guy.' That guy is long gone now. Nobody misses him.

There weren't going to be any wild parties in the co-op I moved into. Everyone who lived there was also a geezer and understood the value of minding their own damn business—a pack of touchy old hippies, punks, and ex-bikers looking out for each other and otherwise staying out of each other's way. The buy-in wasn't exactly cheap, but it was either that, some sort of assisted living crap... or waiting until a real accident took me out.

But it wasn't like I was broke. The pension package from the 'IT consulting firm' I'd retired from was surprisingly decent, thanks to the people I really worked for. The package from the people I really really worked for was better yet—if I needed it. In any case, the rent revenue from my old place on Morningstar's Mountain more than covered my food and booze budget. Other than the fact that it's falling apart, nothing in this world is what it seems.
This goes doubly triply true for me.

After I moved into the coop, I wound up keeping my old Porsche in a garage up the street. Mostly, I just walked. I kept telling myself the walking stick was temporary until my hip got better... but I also knew I was probably bull-shitting myself.

I'd halfway thought about moving back to Texas, but I was used to the Northwest. Also, it was pretty obvious that most of the country had gone completely fucking crazy and was a crisis or two away from a bad replay of Nazi Germany... or a worse replay of the fall of
Rome.

If things did unravel, the choice between winding up in the 'Republic of Texas' or finding myself in some sort of 'Cascadia' was pretty much a no-brainer in my mind. If things went the other way... it wasn't much gonna matter anyhow.

There might've been a few places outside of North America I wouldn't mind seeing or seeing again before dying... but it was hard to convince myself it was worth the risk. Between fires, floods, famine, and the increasing threat of war, it looked like civilization was decaying even faster than I was—that the world was as tired of putting up with humanity as it was tired of putting up with me.

I was still waking up in the night, haunted by thoughts of everything that might've been or should've been. I'd made some fairly bad as well as some fairly unique life choices. I'd survived the consequences a lot longer than I should have... but I still wondered about those other versions of me out there in the multiverse, the ones that made other choices. It didn't help that I knew better than most people that all those other versions of me were just as real as me... and probably a lot happier, for the most part.

My days were occasionally a bit haunted as well. It wasn't all that likely that some old business from my past might show up with a claim on what was left of my life or my soul... but it wasn't impossible. That long-gone guy I used to be had managed to piss off a few folks. And even though most of them have preceded me into hell, the ones that worried me the most were not beyond the occasional day pass.

Old habits die hard. I followed Wild Bill Hickok's advice on the subject of doors and seating, Cagiostro's advice onards of protection, and Kent Allard's advice on just about everything else. Like everyone else in the cosmos, I'm just playing my luck and playing for time. I eventually managed to convince myself that if any of those old markers ever got called in, I would willingly give up—that I would surrender what little life or soul I had left without a fight.

I was wrong.

two: evangeia

I had thought my father was the wisest being in all the worlds.

"My people see it as a duty, Aelia," he had told me. "Very few are so favored by fortune in all the universes, and so we offer guidance and protection to those less favored. The gifts of my people are passed on to you. How you choose to use them is up to you. But to join in the ward-ship of this world would be an honor and a service to both your peoples."

It would be centuries before I realized he was not only wise but also the second-most accomplished liar I have ever known, exceeded only in that art by the ageless being that occasionally humored itself with the name 'Lucifer Morningstar.'

By the time this realization came, I was so bound by the 'wardship of this world' that I could no more set it aside than I might set aside my own life. My determination in this has made me wonder on occasion just how much the 'gifts' of my father's people really had been passed on to me. As humans age, they become stubbornly determined, often in foolish small things. Though I seem to age as my father aged, could my mind—even slightly—be touched by the foibles of an aging human? My physicians say not... but it would explain much.

In some ways, my wardship may soon become much simpler. My mother's people have apparently grown bored with civilization. This is perhaps not a bad thing. Protecting them from being used as cattle by Selenites is a good deal easier when not complicated by the need to protect them and their planet from themselves.

It would have been great good fortune had they grown in stature. My father's folk have few enough allies and are ever in need of more. Perhaps the next time, my mother's people evolve something resembling technology. It will take longer next time, given the resources they've destroyed. Perhaps ten thousand years, perhaps as long as twenty.

Gods help me; I'll probably still be here.

There are times when I miss the days when I could move among my mother's people as a goddess or a spirit. They were simpler and, in some ways, less lonely those days—regardless of the occasional inconvenience of being worshipped or threatened with fire. Only in the most primitive or most advanced parts of my motherworld could I attempt any such thing now... and I suspect I would gain little in return.

There are other times when I cannot help but wonder how else my life might have been, lacking either certain gifts or having not accepted certain obligations. The walls between worlds have not yet thinned so greatly that I could know such things... but I do still wonder.

But only briefly. The worlds are what they are, the choices I made remain—and they are binding. Grief and regret are equally dangerous luxuries I cannot afford. My obligations define me.

I keep them.

three: murphy

Just when I thought I was out, just when it looked like I might get to die peacefully from old age...

Yup. They pulled me back.

It had been a pretty day—rainy and overcast to start out, then the sun came out around noon—and I decided to get out and enjoy it. I'd found a table at a sidewalk café and bought a paper. Sure, there was a tablet in my backpack... but it just ain't the same.

I was working my way through the sports section and considering another dirty chai when a shadow fell across the page. A familiar voice, one I'd not heard in some time, asked, "May I join you?"

"But of course," I gestured to an adjacent empty chair. "Daylight suits you, Evangeia—you oughta try it more often."

The inhumanly tall and eldritchly beautiful woman who used to really really be my boss had not made a personal appearance in a long time... and never once in daylight. I had never really known whether it was theater or some genuine vampire-like aversion to the sun. As far as I know, there ain't no such thing as vampires in the Hollywood sense—but given that I had never been completely clear on just what, exactly, Evangeia de Lourdes actually happened to be... let's just say I would not have been surprised.

On the other hand, having her turn up in a coffee shop in Southeast Portland some decades after my retirement... that part was pretty unexpected. She was wearing a green sun dress that complemented her red hair, a scarf that concealed her not-quite-human ears, and vintage Ray-Bans to mask her not-quite-human eyes. She was even wearing flats on her not-quite-human feet. That she had not visibly aged from our last encounter surprised me not at all.

"Old habits," she said. "My appearance by moonlight is less noteworthy— but even by daylight, I am hardly noteworthy here. This place you now call home is... interesting."

"Portland? It's okay. There's definitely some folks that overdo the 'keep it weird' thing, but they're sincere about it. Hell, you could even lose the scarf and the shades. Folks would just think you were cosplaying."

"Another time, perhaps."

I was trying to figure out where this was going... and why. Once upon a time, I'd been useful. I'd had skills in a variety of dark arts; wound up selling those skills and my loyalties to whoever or whatever wanted to pay my price. The inhuman conspiracy that calls itself 'The Order' had paid best of all and had also made it clear that—whether I played an active role or not—my involvement with them was a lifetime commitment. But the commitment, in my case, was pretty close to being used up. My own usefulness even more so.

"So," I said. "You were checking out the new titles at Powell's, fancied a coffee, saw an old friend, thought you'd amble over and say 'howdy'... right?"

"Not entirely. I prefer the original location."

"Yeah, me too. I'm still more than happy to spring for a beverage. These guys stock that herbal tea you used to be partial to—but if you want to spike it with Benedictine, you're on your own."

"Kind of you, but not necessary. This is no social call."

"I didn't really think that you'd come all the way over from—well, wherever the hell it is you come from—just to see me. But I'm having a hard time seeing much other reason."

"How so?"

"Evangeia, in case you hadn't noticed, I'm old, useless, and used up. There is not a single thing you or anyone else would ask me to do that someone else can't do better."

"And if that were not the case?"

"The 'used up' part would still apply."

"Perhaps less than you think." She reached into her purse and gave me a wax-sealed parchment envelope. "There is a need for you—and an opportunity, should you want it. Some things are best shared by moonlight. Two nights hence, be at the place and time named here if you would like to know more... or not. The choice is yours."

four: evangeia

What my father had described as a 'duty' would've been perfectly understandable to any Roman officer in Gaul, any British officer in Bengal, or any American officer in Iraq. So, as well would've been the propensity for dallying with the local females... but that is another story.

When the walls between worlds had first grown thin, my father's folk had already been in possession of advanced technology, including space travel. They had colonized the worlds of their own solar system and began to cast eyes outward, wondering how to bridge the unimaginable gulf between stars.

Then they found there was no such need—that across other dimensions other than space, other worlds were far closer.

They formed a civilization like no other, a culture like no other. Fortune had favored my father's folk with a greater cosmos, my mother's world one among many. They found resources. They found allies.

They also found a threat.

I will always think of them as 'Selenites,' having seen firsthand the infestations of their hives on Earth's moon. They have as many names as do my father's folk... but a single purpose. Seldom is that purpose expressed in words, but
I have seen the remains of worlds where it had been expressed in deeds.

Containing that purpose became the fundamental purpose of my father's folk.

The war to control the greater cosmos touched every part of that greater cosmos, including my mother's 'Earth'—my homeworld that I eventually swore to protect. The scars of that struggle have mostly faded from my mother's world, but memory of it lives on in the folklore and myth of my mother's people.

The Selenites are utterly ancient, utterly alien, utterly voracious. They travel between universes in ways we do not, perhaps, cannot understand. They infest worlds, and they harvest them. Even in worlds where they have been otherwise contained, sentients and beasts alike sometimes simply become... missing, sometimes later found mad or mutilated. The purpose served is unknown. My mother's people now call these predations 'abduction' when they know of it at all. One purpose of my wardship is to ensure they know as little of this as possible. They are not ready.

My father's folk began exploring their universe at a time when my mother's people were finding uses for chipped flint. But the Selenites first left their own homeworld when all of my ancestor's ancestors were swimming in various primeval oceans and growing spinal cords. Little wonder they see all others as feedstock or slaves.
It is not possible to bargain with them. They can only be resisted.

Whether by evolution or by choice, they are hive creatures—either unable or unwilling to communicate with individual minds. If those hive minds are as well parts of a greater whole, that collective conscious is one of the oldest sentient beings in all of the greater cosmos.

But not the oldest.

* * * *

It calls itself 'Morningstar,' among many other things. If the tales of its creation are true, it has been continually conscious since this universe began. But all of these are tales told by Morningstar, and therein lies a problem.

Because Morningstar lies.

Whether the literal fallen angel of its own telling or simply some primordial remnant of an earlier cosmic era, it had dwelt on my mother's world long before my father's folk arrived. The thing we found here claimed it had been here for many millions of years, which may even be true. Regardless, thousands more years passed before it became known to us.

Once known, it was left unmolested. My father's folk are pragmatists. The wardship of my mother's world was neither helped nor hindered by the presence of this thing. It was neither friend nor foe, ally nor adversary. And if any of the tales it told for its own amusement were anything other than lies, Morningstar might well have adversaries of its own—adversaries far more dangerous than any Selenite.

So Morningstar was left to wander among my mother's people. When came the time to conceal from them the existence of a greater cosmos, there was no need to conceal Morningstar; it concealed itself. I am enough my mother's child to be intrigued by this thing, enough my father's daughter to seek a use for it. Finding none, I followed the pragmatism of my father's folk.

That all ended when Morningstar became the adversary of my adversaries—if not quite an ally. When came the opportunity for it to end its exile, the warders of my mother's world found no reason to interfere.

13

The question of what Morningstar truly was ceased to matter when Morningstar's exile ended. Friend or foe, ally or adversary, angel or demon or mad elder god... it all ceased to matter when Morningstar passed beyond mortal reckoning on reborn wings of fire.

Or so we thought.

five: murphy

I had first met Evangeia decades earlier, back in Houston, at a party in an old mansion near Rice University. I was distributing LSD to party guests, and my first thought upon seeing her was that I had screwed up and accidentally dosed myself. By the end of the evening, I knew she was real... and that my hosts were into some really strange shit.

Then I found out just how strange shit could be—but that's another story.

I was a feckless and fearless little monster back then who firmly believed the world owed him a thing or two. I'd recently brokered hacking skills and a capacity for casual violence into a subcontracting gig for what people like me liked to call 'The Company.' It had been a nice step up from dealing drugs and throwing people out of clubs... but nothing compared to the offer I accepted that moonless night.

It's called a lot of things. I learned to just call it 'The Order'—and learned also not to talk about it. Being initiated into a hidden conspiracy of occultists and not-quite-human beings is nothing like being hired as a bagman for a government-sanctioned criminal enterprise... except when it is.

In both cases, a mistake can get you killed—or worse than killed. In both cases, you learn that the real world isn't really 'real' at all... just a convenient and comforting lie. Conspiracies exploit that lie, but no conspiracy ever created it. The lie is as old as human consciousness.

Basically, it is human consciousness.

The cover story within a cover story within the cover story of who and what I really am started out complicated and got worse. But keeping the books on drug deals in my head had also been complicated, so had writing code and casting spells. 'Complicated' is something I've always been good at.

I also learned a long time ago that a plausible anomaly works just fine as a cover story as long as it's plausible. As long as people want to be lied to, 'plausible' will always be good enough—and people always want to be lied to. It all worked until I fell in love. That, too, is another story. Let's just say that whatever I ever thought the world owed me has been paid back in pain... and with interest.

I had no damned idea why Evangeia de Lourdes was turning up again, years after I'd retired from the strange shit she'd initiated me into. I had a few ideas what the bribe might be for whatever it was they wanted me to do. If it was what I suspected, not many people would turn it down. The problem is that I'm not 'many people'—I'm just the one sad/wise old fuck who knows better than most that there ain't no such thing as a free lunch.

I knew that if I didn't go, it would be the end of it. I'm pretty far past my 'sell-by' date. My various former employers were all pretty clear on that concept, whatever Evangeia might think. Whether I lingered on another five years or another ten—or more, if I was 'lucky'—I would be permitted the dignity I wasn't even sure I deserved: Living out my life and dying in peace. Which was almost certainly the smart play.

I also knew that if I didn't go, I'd spend that five or ten or however many years kicking myself and wondering what I'd missed out on—and I've got too many regrets already. I didn't need another reason to wake up in the night staring into a darkness that stared back. Not only that, I had nothing left to lose. I even remotely came close to giving a damn about.

I was reasonably fond of my housemates, but very few of us were willing to be much more than friends. I had other friends as well, in the various parts of the Northwest I'd called 'home' one time or another... even a few that might miss me once I was finally gone. I'd once had cats that were the closest thing to family once my real family was gone—but once they were gone as well, I decided not to replace them. Losing them had felt too much like losing my mom and dad.

Somewhere out there was a woman I'd once been willing to rebuild my life for, but she had decided a long time ago that she could and would seek better options. I still think the option she wound up with is a bit of a fucking joke. One reason among many we don't talk anymore.

I watched Evangeia walk away up Hawthorne Street until she wasn't there any more. Her comings and goings by moonlight tended to be more picturesque, but I hadn't expected anything like that in daylight on a busy street. I blinked—possibly had been made to blink—and she was gone.

When I ordered that second dirty chai I'd been thinking about. I was tempted to ask the waitress to describe the woman who had stopped briefly at my table... but only a little. I had found out a long time ago that the less I knew about how much other people really knew about the strange shit that occasionally happens to me, the better.

It was not unlikely that the answer might be, "what woman?" which would reopen a debate I've been lucky enough not to have with myself for close to a couple of decades. It had been kind of fun, being able to simply take for granted what was and was not real. I can see why most people prefer it that way.

Too bad I'm not one of them.

Even though I'm retired from it all, I can't pick up a newspaper without finding myself trying to parse out the relative portions of truth, disinformation, and pure bullshit. The fact that what's 'true' is bullshit—and more so, every single day—doesn't make it any easier. Writing the disinformation had once been one of the things I'd been paid to do. The fact that I'd been producing different levels of disinformation at once for different organizations had been challenging... but not much more than any of the other complicated things I'd managed to get good at.

I very much doubted that I was going to be called out of retirement to write press releases. The world isn't what it used to be. The base-level absurdity of what now passes for 'real' has all but eliminated any need for The Order to conceal its existence at all.

It was even less likely that what Evangeia had in mind involved the sort of hands-on stuff that had more or less started my career. The last time I punched someone, they actually got back up again. Shortly after that... I stopped punching people.

Whatever this was about, it was going to involve the 'strange shit' part of my resume—the really strange shit. That strange shit had made my life interesting, but it had also sort of ruined it. I'd eventually learned how to be normal, learned how to not have secrets.

The ones I'd kept had cost me greatly.

I swilled down the rest of my chai, put a couple of bills under the empty glass, stood up, and shouldered my backpack. I could put off opening that parchment envelope until after I got home. It was still a beautiful day. The mysteries and moonlight could wait.

six: evangeia

Eons ago, my father's folk had sought to explore the universe.

They found a multiverse instead... but not an infinite one. There are places where space is more than empty, where the void itself opens to a deeper void. Through higher dimensions, these rifts bridge million-year gaps in probability space—the gap between a universe where my father's folk traveled between planets and a universe where my mother's people hunted mammoths, or the gap between either of those and a universe where intelligent saurians took the place of any hominid... or the even greater gap bridged to a universe where hives of humanoid insects acquired the appetite to consume worlds.

These more than empty places occur as universes expand and the fabric of their spacetime grows thin. Sometimes, those thin spots are congruent, and a rift occurs. But it is a rare and recent thing: not all universes expand; those that do expand at differing rates. Not all universes obligingly place an 'Earth' in the vicinity of such rifts.

It happens often enough, though. My father's folk found a greater cosmos of conjoined universes, each with its own Earth, each Earth home to at least one species that had evolved into intelligence. My father's folk were not alone in this discovery. Others, as well, knew of the greater cosmos had as well the means to traverse the places where space is more than empty.

And eventually found themselves with a common enemy.

In their own universe, it is believed that nothing any longer exists other than the Selenites themselves. What else explains the voracity with which they prey upon the rest of the greater cosmos? Having depleted a universe, they now seek to consume others.

The stable alliance against them has held for many thousands of years. Worlds harvested by them are worlds the alliance destroys. Knowing this, they limit their predations. Whatever they may do in their own universe or elsewhere is unknowable. In the known greater cosmos, Selenites are contained.

But now, the greater cosmos itself is changing.

The walls between worlds are growing thinner. Where once the rifts only connected across million-year gaps in probability, now they bridge gaps measured in mere millennia. The process itself seems to be accelerating for reasons we can only speculate upon.

For my father's folk and the ones I serve, this is both threat and opportunity. The thinned walls between worlds means more worlds Selenites can attempt to harvest, but it also means more worlds in which those opposed to them can find allies.

Other threats, other opportunities are also possible. The greater cosmos is expanding. So far, no new crosstime-capable species have revealed themselves, but it is only a matter of time. The unknowable totality of the true multiverse contains everything.

Even a slight expansion of the greater cosmos toward that totality could undo everything my father's folk had ever built, could unravel the alliance against the Selenites, could expose us to things far worse.

Already, it exposed us to a threat we had thought ended.

* * * *

The wardship of my mother's world requires much. Above all else, it requires secrecy.

Even now, they are not ready. My mother's people are inventive, cruel, generous, spiteful. They have all but laid waste to their own world. They dream—as did my father's folk—of spreading to other worlds through space. The knowledge that other worlds are already far closer is not knowledge with which they can be trusted.

They have not always been warded in secret, but they are now. The role I have played in warding them has changed many times involved many tools. The best tool now is their own tendency for keeping secrets—and recruiting agents from within those keepers of secrets.

Recruiting Murphy had been a gamble, but one in which we'd risked little. At the right time and in the right place, he'd possessed abilities that are not common in my mother's people—and so we used him. We had hoped he might advance further in the organization I recruited him from, but he advanced sufficiently to be of continued use.

And now... he was useful again. I had been empowered to offer him much. Assuming he lived, he would be earning every bit of it.

seven: murphy

The 'particular place' in Evangeia's note was across the river, high in Portland's West Hills. The 'particular time' was, unsurprisingly, moonrise. I parked the old Porsche on a nearby residential street and hiked the rest of the way. I was leaning pretty heavily on my hiking pole, but not so much that I was worried about falling and not getting up. It had been a nice drive getting there. The winding road to the park reminded me a lot of the home I'd left behind in a neighboring state, on a midget mountain where I'd once met a fallen angel.

Meeting someone who convincingly claimed to be Lucifer himself had been an interesting conclusion to an interesting career. Helping him end his exile upon Earth had been profitable and enlightening. Even though I only knew and fought beside him for a few days, the impact of that meeting changed my life more than I realized at the time. At the very least, befriending the cosmic embodiment of loss, disappointment, and pain had given perspective to my own.

But this, too, is another story.

Council Crest Park is one of the highest points in the city. The only thing higher is a big red and white radio transmitter to the immediate southeast called Stonehenge Tower. This particular hilltop had been used for public meetings before us white assholes showed up and ruined the neighborhood; that's why it's 'Council' Crest. You can see all the way to Mount Rainier in good weather, with downtown Portland laid out like a jewel at your feet.

It was a clear night. I picked a bench with a nice view to the north and watched the air traffic flying in and out of PDX. Of course, I wasn't particularly surprised when a light came in over the airport and kept flying in my direction. Nor was I surprised to find myself alone in the park. These things just sort of happen.

At the appointed time, the light grew rapidly from a gleaming point to a silver convex disc, its lower half glowing from within like mother of pearl. I knew there would be no UFO report. Craft of The Order are stealthed in multiple ways, including the psychic. Once, there had been other visitors on this world not quite so stealthy.

Explaining them away had once been one of my jobs.

The job pretty much went away after I retired... at least in part because so had most of the visitors.

The glowing silver disk slowed, orbited the park, and then came to rest directly above me. An opening grew in the glowing lower half. A Thing that looked like a gargoyle with Yiddish graffiti etched into its skull bounded like a dog down an artificial moonbeam that was suddenly there and sat on a nearby picnic table.

"Hi, Jocephus," I said. "Been a while."

"Indeed," replied the Thing.

Then Evangeia made a similar descent, joining me on my bench. She was attired after the manner of her people for a change in what looked like a highcollared pale gray flight suit. "Quite a nice view from this place," she said.
"I am glad you came, Murphy."

"Beats checkers at the senior center all to blazes," I said. "So what's up?"

"There are some things I wish to show you. Can you take a short trip?"

"I left my car parked in front of someone's house a few blocks from here."

"We can pick it up on the way."

* * * *

The craft of The Order decloaked. "So," I asked. "Where are we?"

"I believe you would describe this as the current 'Area Fifty Whatever,'" Evangeia replied.

"I was thinking that might be the case," I told her. "But where is it?"

"Apologies—Greenland. Given the current political climate, The Order no longer considers the continental United States a safe location for sensitive operations."

"The Order is hardly alone in that assessment," I replied. "Then this is not a U.S.-operated facility?"

"No. It is not." Evangeia and I were seated in the back of her craft's flight deck. Before us, the craft's pilot—a human woman, also in a gray jumpsuit—went about the work of landing us. On a view screen before us, our destination became clear as it came closer.

Soon, we were landed on a rock shelf over the base proper, lined up with other craft of The Order. Then we descended a bridge of moonbeams to the base itself.

The base was a remnant from the US/USSR Cold War—aging quonset huts surrounding an airstrip, repurposed for the needs of The Order. On the other side of the airstrip stood a cluster of much newer geodesic domes.
That is where we descended.

"What I am going to share with you now, you will likely find displeasing," Evangeia said. "And for that, I am sorry. But it is necessary. Necessary that you know why we have reached out to you."

"I'm a big boy," I told her. "And this is far from my first rodeo."

* * * *

The interior of the dome was a hodgepodge of human and not-human technology. A lot of the human tech seemed medical in nature. The base staff was a mix of humans and Evangeia's people, along with a few Sauroids in security roles, as well as what appeared to be robots.

At the center of the dome was a smaller dome—opaque and equipped with an airlock. A 'clean room,' it would seem, from the rack of suits next to the airlock.

"Please put one of these on," Evangeia said as she donned a suit of her own. Jocephus remained at the airlock door as we entered.

Inside, even more medical tech. At the very center, the reason for it.

What had once been a human body hung suspended in a web of force, connected by a multitude of tubes and wires to the surrounding equipment. Parts of the body seemed atrophied and twisted, and other parts had grown. It seemed unlikely that the being I saw could have stood or walked unassisted. Despite the transformation, I could tell that the body belonged to someone who'd once been a friend... of sorts.

"Hello, Murphy," said the thing that had once been Colvin Case. Unsurprisingly, the voice was hoarse and husky. "They said you'd be coming to see me."

"That's more than they told me." Colvin Case had been my friend and later my boss back when I worked for The Company. Later still, he'd been revealed as one of the Greys' deepcover genetic experiments. I hadn't really believed he was a hybrid when I found out.

I believed it now.

Describing his complexion as 'ashen' would constitute an understatement. His hair was thinner than ever, or maybe what had happened to his skull just made it seem that way. The eyes were the same, though.

When we parted years before, it hadn't exactly been on good terms. He had used psychic powers I'd not known he had, used them on me in a way that I might be inclined to call 'torture.' I wound up threatening to blow his head apart with a high-caliber handgun... having recently done the same to several of his masters.

"Typical," he said. "They may look more human but don't be fooled. Your friends are just as inclined to see you and I as cattle or foot soldiers as the ones who made me."

"I'm not so sure about the 'cattle' part, but point taken otherwise."

"They haven't told you, have they?"

"I haven't been told much of anything yet. Told me what?"

"Apparently, we get to work together again," he chuckled huskily. "You and I are the key components in an exciting new technology, old buddy. We're going to go huntingangels."

* * * *

Next to the inner dome, there was what looked like a break room of sorts, complete with a coffee maker. I sat at one of the tables. Evangeia joined me after retrieving two paper cups from a dispenser. She then produced a silver flask from a pocket of her jumpsuit. "Brandy?"

"Absolutely," I replied. It wasn't as good as the stuff Morningstar used to drink, but it definitely hit the spot under present circumstances. "Hunting angels?" I asked.

"Just the one angel, really... the one you've met."

I laughed and pointed in a random direction. "Unless he had a warp drive in his pocket he didn't want to talk about. Lucifer Morningstar is the better part of 20 light-years distant that way."

"In a way—but in another way, much closer."

"No riddles, Evangeia, no 'oracles.' I'm old, and I'm tired, and you want something. Best you tell me what that something is."

"Of course." She poured us both more brandy. "Your friend Morningstar is flying through deep space at relativistic speeds for one simple reason: the Selenites wanted him badly enough to bait a trap for him with something almost as uniquely powerful and valuable as Morningstar himself."

"Not quite," I said. "He's flying home to God because that's what he wants to do. He gets to do it because your masters decided it was safer to let that happen than take a chance on the Greys—sorry, 'Selenites'—making another play for him."

"Your masters also, Murphy—but you are otherwise correct. We have only suspicions of why the Selenites wanted Morningstar, but it does not truly matter. They are devourers of worlds. No purpose of theirs is one we can trust."

"So I have been told," I said, "from the day you initiated me."

"Do you feel you have been misinformed?"

I laughed. "Everyone I ever worked for told me what they thought I 'needed to know' and not one damned thing more. I'm sure that everything The Order has ever told me about Selenites is just as operationally correct as anything The Company ever told me about the 'evil empire' they were at war with. The only difference is that in your case, I pretty much have to take it at face value—I'm only human, after all."

"What you have been told is not merely 'operationally' correct, Murphy, although your cynicism is entirely understandable. You were permitted to help Morningstar. We permitted him to leave. We had to make sure Morningstar—or any like him—remained utterly beyond the reach of Selenites."

"Archangel or not, I don't think he needed your 'permission' to leave Earth—or that not having it would've made much difference."

Evangeia looked into her brandy for a long moment.
Once again, I found myself wondering what she really was, what had ever drawn anything like her into my world. All I really knew about Morningstar was what he'd told me over a couple of days. Over a couple of decades, Evangeia had told me a little more of her own true nature. I've been lied to for my own good, lied to for the hell of it, and lied to by people so high on their own shit they actually thought it was true.

'Cynical'? Yeah, maybe... and maybe for a good reason or two.

Then she looked up. "'Angel' is as good a term as any for what he was and the term he preferred. 'Dawn Matter entity' is a close translation of what my... people have termed him. You are probably correct that we could not truly have hindered him. It was best, in any case, that he simply leave. Better still that no others like him present the same risk."

"So this," I said, "is why you are calling me out of retirement—so I can go 'hunting angels' with that thing in the next room? He don't look very portable... and in case you've not noticed, I'm kinda past this sort of thing."

"Not quite," Evangeia said. "Case will remain where he is for the rest of his life... which will continue just as long as we have need of him. A great deal has happened since your retirement, Murphy, including things someone like you would typically not know of. Things I must try to tell you now."

"You mean my 'need to know' just escalated?"

"I fear so."

eight: evangeia

They suspect the existence of a greater cosmos—that much is obvious.

The folklore and shared fantasies of my mother's people have grown, mutated, metastasized. The lies and halftruths their world's warders have told them are woven into the massive web of lies they tell themselves. That constructed reality is now more valuable to them than reality itself. They are now as likely to die drowning in dreams as they are to die from poisoning their own planet.

In either case... they will die dreaming of other worlds.

As an initiate of The Order, Murphy knew more than most of the greater cosmos. It was now time for him to know still more.

"How much do you truly know about the rifts between worlds?" In addition to a break area, the space outside Case's containment also included a conference room. Switching from brandy to coffee, I conducted Murphy to a seat in that room.

"I know they exist," Murphy said. "I know your people and a few others know how to use them. I know that Greys can even create them. Morningstar told me the rifts are a recent thing... at least by his standards."

"All of this is true," I told him. "What you do not know is that my people now have as well the ability to create rifts—but what we are now able to do is not what the Selenites do. The rifts we create are barely above subatomic in size. Anything larger, anything comparable to portals created by Selenites, would have power requirements comparable to the energy output of entire galaxies.

"But in learning to do even this, we have confirmed a thing long suspected: neither we nor the Selenites can open artificial portals—by any means—between universes not already connected. The portals can only be opened between universes for which natural rifts already occur."

"Do you know why?" Murphy asked.

"We do not. It is a function of some higher-order reality we cannot access. But we know it to be true.

"Know this as well," I told him. "The rifts themselves are changing. When my people first learned of them, the places we could access were millions of years apart in probability space. Now, the rifts that occur naturally can open across mere tens of thousands of crosstime years—in some cases, even less. This is potentially a serious problem. Do you see it?"

Murphy frowned. "I can see a few problems. More rifts means more visitors from other worlds—maybe to the point that it's finally time to give up the cover-up... tell humanity what 'flying saucers' really are.

"If I thought civilization on this Earth was gonna last long enough for my own people to discover rift travel, I could see us being a problem—but I don't think either you or I think that's gonna happen."

"Actually," I said, "Your analysis does you credit. Those are indeed potential issues. But we feel there may be a more immediate matter, a threat transcending this one mere Earth.

"In theory, every single discrete moment of time spawns an entire separate universe for every single outcome of that moment, which would make the multiverse an infinitely dimensioned matrix of infinite parallel universes. No such thing has ever been observed; there are differing opinions on whether this is even true.

"Even though the walls between worlds grow thin, they are not yet so thin that you could meet an alternate version of yourself... but if you were immortal and very old, that might not be the case. Do you see it now?"

"Morningstar," Murphy said. "Morningstar, or others like him."

"Exactly. Morningstar described himself as made of 'Dawn Matter,' a remnant of the early days of creation. Twice, Selenites attempted his abduction—once centuries ago, then the attempt you helped foil. They have made no significant incursions upon this Earth since that attempt, but nothing else has changed. We've no reason to believe they would not try again... given the chance."

"And that chance now exists?" Murphy asked.

"It does."

Murphy glared at me. "If this is going where I think it's going, you have plumb lost your half-space-alien mind, Evangeia. Even if I were inclined and able, what could you possibly offer to make any such thing worth my while?"

I knew that he knew. He had served us too long to not suspect had known of too many others who had received the same payment for services rendered. The only real question was if he would deem the payment sufficient. Some did not. It had taken many centuries for me to understand this: Sometimes, my mother's people embrace the short span of their existence.

One word would confirm what he suspected.

"Life."

nine: murphy

Just when I thought I was out, they pulled me back... with an offer I couldn't refuse.

I'd heard rumors for years—but really, the rumor of an elixir vitae had gone back centuries. I'd never met anyone who would admit to having been offered such a thing had been even less certain I'd take it if the offer was made. The few occasions I'd ever met the 'people' Evangeia reported up to, my impression was that it didn't particularly matter whether they were ascended humans, space alien hybrids, robots in disguise, or all of the above—they were coldly inhuman on a level I had no interest in reaching. I would live or die as a man, dammit.

Only now, 'dying' was less abstract to me than it had ever been before.

I had closed out my home, sold or stored most of my things, and gone to live with a community of people united by one thing alone: The imminence of death, the desire to live life as best they could, knowing that time was short. I hadn't been diagnosed with any particular disease, but I knew someday I'd screw up, do something I would've once recovered from, and that would be the end of it. As I had once made peace with loneliness after my wife left me, I would now make peace with death.

Only to discover I could do no such damned thing. And unlike 99% or so of humanity, I was being offered a choice.

"I haven't said 'yes' to one goddam thing," I told Evangeia. "But just how, exactly, does this work?"

We'd moved from the break room to a conference room that could've been in any office park anywhere on earth. At least the chairs were more comfortable.

"It works by rewriting your DNA, more or less, into a configuration approximating mine."

"You mean I get pointy ears?"

"The cosmetic changes are neither that extreme nor immediate. When the process works, other changes are. That hiking stick you use as a cane would become unnecessary almost immediately. Within months, you would find yourself much as you were when we first initiated you."

"When you guys first 'initiated' me, I was a cocky little bastard with a mohawk moving coke for The Company and throwing people out of clubs for fun and profit. Hopefully, you don't mean that literally—and what do you mean 'when the process works'?"

"There remains a remote chance it would not work at all, a more remote chance you would not survive the process—it has happened before. As for the rest..." Evangeia raised one perfect eyebrow. "What you do with your rejuvenation, once you have done as we ask, is entirely up to you."

"How long would I live?"

"It's impossible to say. All humans are different. Decades, to be sure, that you would otherwise not have. Perhaps much more."

"That's assuming I manage to live through whatever it is you guys have in mind," I told her. "It's about time you got to that part, Evangeia. Be sure to include the stuff about why it's me doing this, as opposed to some guy recently recruited from Special Ops you don't have to bribe with—oh, fuck me. Immortality, more or less."

"It's complicated," she said.

"Apparently, I have time."

ten: evangeia

In the aftermath of the Selenite incursion Murphy helped end, my organization's priorities shifted.

Protecting Murphy's version of Earth became less a concern. Not only had the Selenites withdrawn, other crosstime species were departing as well. Other Earths meant other opportunities—either worlds not infested with creatures like my mother's people or perhaps versions of them less inclined toward their own destruction.

A new priority became what the Case hybrid described as 'hunting angels.' We could no longer afford to treat Morningstar as an eccentric elder being best left to amuse himself among mortals. We could not simply assume that no others of his kind lay within the Selenites' grasp. We had to know.

Also a priority: trying to determine why the Selenites had gone to such lengths to abduct Morningstar in the first place. The first attempt had been a mystery and perhaps even an error—and whether or not the Selenites had intended the abduction of an archangel, the result of that attempt had made plain the consequences. The second attempt had involved resources comparable to harvesting a world. If 'Dawn Matter' mattered so greatly... we had to know why.

The first priority proved more accessible than the second. My people have been attempting to decode Selenite technology since roughly the time of Earth's last major ice age. While much of what has come within our grasp has yielded secrets, much more has not. In the aftermath of the second attempt to take Morningstar, we had two more pieces of technology to work with: Case himself and several devices disguised as .45 caliber bullets—devices with a unique and specific effect on a Dawn Matter entity such as Morningstar.

It took time, but eventually, we had what we wanted: Call it a 'Dawn Matter detector.'

Mutating the Case hybrid into a form more similar to those who had made him had unlocked sensory abilities close to their own. Cybernetic augments to his nervous system kept those abilities under our control. Case could now detect the presence of Dawn Matter—not just on this Earth, but its close alternates as well. What we found as a result was reassuring in some ways and challenging in others.

And also surprising.

"So, it's another version of Morningstar?" Murphy asked me.

"We don't know that as a certainty, but it seems likely. Had any other of his kind been close at hand in this or adjacent universes, we would have known already. We do know that this is the only such signature to be found in nearby probability space."

"And the universe he's in is somehow something new?"

That was the surprising part. We knew the walls between worlds had grown thin—but not so thin as this. The universe our detector pointed to was... an anomaly.

"It's a universe, no more new or old than any other. But it should not be where we found it. And the 'Earth' we discovered inside it is unique to my people's experience."

There is no exact way to determine the point of diversion between the different Earths we find in probability space. Comparative DNA analysis between my mother's and father's people pinpoints our worlds' divergence with some accuracy. Similar techniques have established the divergence between most of the known universes containing lifeforms that travel between them.

No such technique would be of any use in the universe the Dawn Matter detector had found.

"You're shitting me, right?" Murphy said. "Time travel?"

"Only in effect," I told him. "As near as we can determine, the Earth we found is a close analog to your own—give or take what appears to be a few decades."

"Any theories on this?"

"None," I told him. "The only reason my people discovered the rifts in the first place was because we were trying to travel between stars—the discovery, for us, was essentially an accident. Everything we know about the structure of the multiverse is from observational data acquired over centuries... this is new data acquired under fairly novel circumstances."

"Yeah, no shit." Murphy shuddered. "Case has been wired up like that... for how long?"

"For many years. What was done was necessary."

"I've heard that one before... but I suppose, in this case, you're probably right."

"We are," I told him. "Thanks to our work since your retirement with the hybrid you know as 'Case,' we think we now know what the Selenites hoped to achieve... and why."

"I've wondered about that," Murphy said. "Seemed like an awful lot of work for an awfully thin payoff. Granted, the little grey bastards get up into some strange shit."

"They are strange to others," I said. "But that strangeness conceals purpose. There is circumstantial evidence that Morningstar's long tenure upon this Earth may have contributed locally to the weakened walls between worlds. We think the Selenites aim to weaken them even more."

"To what end?" Murphy asked.

"The only end they ever have: more worlds to infest and feed upon."

"That would make sense. Why do you think Morningstar's 'long tenure' has weakened the walls between worlds here on Earth?"

"Because we know the large number of transdimensional rifts in the near vicinity of Earth is a local phenomenon. Practical interstellar travel is an impossibility, but my kind have been in space for a long time—long enough to send probes to other star systems. We know that what occurs in the near vicinity of Earth does not occur in any other star system we know of in any of the universes we have yet reached. Earth is a crossroads within crosstime, fundamentally unique. We have never understood why. We think, perhaps, we now do."

"Have there been any noticeable changes since Morningstar left?"

"No, but he was here for millions of years. A mere decade or two may be insufficient."

"It's not much less improbable than anything else I've lived through since we first met," Murphy said. "Assuming—no offense—you're not lying to me.

"I appreciate this thorough briefing, Evangeia, but you've managed to leave out the two most important parts: the part about what—exactly—you plan to do when someone finds your 'angel,' and the even more important part, at least to me. I'd kind of like to know why that 'someone' needs to be me. If I was recruiting for this gig, I'd be looking for some ex-military a third my age with a dieselpunk fetish."

"I beg pardon?"

"Let me rephrase," Murphy said. "The Order has access to many other potential volunteers eminently better suited for this mission than myself, many of whom would jump at the chance.

"Again: Why me?"

"Such knowledge," I said, "may be less useful than you think; it is not your world's past, for all it is a close analog. In any case, such a person would lack critical attributes in which you are somewhat unique."

"I still haven't committed to one single goddam thing... but tell me more."

"I can actually show you," I told him.

eleven: murphy

I sat and watched the craft of The Order shrink to a dot, then become a reverse shooting star. After, I started the old Porsche and headed back to my garage. I'd talked Evangeia into dropping me off at Mount Tabor, this time, on my side of the river. It worked as well for her purposes, cut my travel time home in half.

In the end, I had to say, "Let me think about it." It was just too damned much.

For decades, I had helped both The Company and The Order conceal from humanity at large different levels of an expanded reality I barely understood myself. Now, the shadowmasters were sharing their secrets and inviting me further into a world I'd thought I'd left behind.

Thanks to the second worst day of my fucking life.

* * * *

The movies get it all wrong. The secret conspiracy between humans and off-world aliens sources 90% of its gear from Amazon, just like the rest of us. Except for the forcefield holding him up, none of the gear in Case's clean room was anything you couldn't find in any hospital or research lab anywhere on the planet. The conference room I was sitting in could've been in any office park anywhere on Earth—even though I'd ridden in a flying

saucer to get there.

The flat-screen TV at the end of the conference table could've been the one sitting in the living room of my seniors' co-op back in Portland. The tablet Evangeia had hooked up to it looked like it could've come from any random electronics store, but I knew it wasn't. That's the other part the movies get wrong. When the secret conspiracy does wind up with a piece of tech from its off-world benefactors, it winds up disguised as something more ordinary.

Sort of like me, for all those years.

Some things are less disguised. The conference room did not have a ceiling and was as brightly lit as a stadium by the lights clustering at the top of the dome. In such light, Evangeia's high cheekbones and obliquely angled eyes, more clearly than ever, were not entirely human. Her hair was a coppery tint mixed with deep magenta. I remembered well from my old punk rock days... but no dye had caused that color. It matched well with the gray jumpsuit she had chosen for the occasion. But the bright lights also made clear a faint dusting of freckles I'd never noticed before—made clear how much she was at least partly human as well.

The screen at the end of the table lit up with what looked like the feed from a surveillance camera.

The scene seemed very familiar.

"I believe you will recognize the date/time stamp," Evangeia said. "This file was retrieved from the Black Rock Containment Facility roughly a decade and a half ago."

"Also known as 'Area Fifty Whatever.' Yeah, I recognize it."

Numerous nonhumans pointing weapons at each other from opposing ends of a long corridor. In the middle of the corridor, a standoff between two apparent humans, also armed. One gestures at the other, who then falls.

"Yourself," Evangeia said. "And Colvin Case."

"Never seen it from this angle," I said. "But yeah... pretty much."

"He entered your mind," Evangeia said.

"It was what I would be inclined to describe as forced entry. I came close to killing him for it."

"Nonetheless, there remains a psychic bond that exists in few other cases."

"If what you propose depends upon renewing that bond, you are shit out of luck," I said. "Even the lure of immortality has its limits."

"What is proposed has no such dependency. Under the magical law of contagion, that bond has never ceased. It can function as what might be described as a 'carrier wave' for what we actually have in mind: using Case's abilities to pinpoint the Dawn Matter detected on this crosstime world and direct you to it. We have the ability to send transmissions through the stable micro rift now open across probability space into that world. You would be able to receive them."

"There's just one last thing you haven't shown me or told me. What's the point of all this? Why are we 'hunting angels?'"

"The only reason that makes any sense," Evangeia replied. "In order to set them free."

* * * *

There was more, of course, but no one was going to share the operational details until I agreed to go. Not only did I need to well and truly think about it, I needed to set my affairs in order.

It wasn't inherently a one-way trip. There was a way to return, if I wanted, the option of staying if I wanted. There was also the slight but real possibility that the rejuvenation therapy would kill me outright or turn me into something that made what was left of Case look downright pretty.

I needed to weigh a literal universe of unknowns against the occasionally comforting known reality of a finite existence that I had come to accept was drawing to a close. If I was careful, I might make it another 10 or 20 years. Or I could get run over by a streetcar as soon as I got back to Portland, just like anyone else.

In any case, it was not a lifetime offer. I was given a simple business card with an email address and a phone number. For two weeks, I would be able to call, text, or email the words "I accept" and receive pickup instructions. After that, the numbers wouldn't work. If anyone tried to use the numbers who wasn't me, the numbers wouldn't work. Based on past experience, I would expect the card to somehow vanish when I wasn't looking if not used in the allotted time—the same way I would've disappeared a long time ago, if I wasn't good at keeping secrets.

"I understand better than most," Evangeia said, "why you might decline this opportunity. Had it ever been possible, I might well have declined my own long existence—had I known what it would entail. And so I understand as well that this is nothing taken lightly. But I shall need your answer soon. And I promise you: in no event shall we ever ask more."

We were once again in the 'flying saucer' that had brought me, piloted by the same unsmiling woman who may or may not have been a local contractor like me—or who may not have really been human at all. On the screen before us, mountains came into view and fell away. I would soon be back in Oregon. "I appreciate that," I said.

Not long after, I found myself watching a distant silver dot most people would call a flying saucer ascending back into the problematic place it had come from. Clouds were rolling in to obscure the moon, and I felt a cool, damp breeze on the back of my neck. Stopping off somewhere for a drink sounded good, but drinking at home sounded even better.

It's called 'being old.'

My phone started buzzing as soon as I turned it back on, but I figured whatever it was could wait until I arrived.

It was perhaps an hour later by the time I had driven back into my neighborhood, parked the car at my garage, and walked home. It was late, I didn't expect anyone else to be awake.

I was wrong.

The seniors' co-op I'd bought into was a big, rambling house on the end of a quiet street. Even though the living room was a common area that any resident could use any time they wanted, the reality is that we're a bunch of geezers who tend to go to bed early. Not this time—the entire house was brightly lit.

"This can't be good," I said to no one in particular.

It wasn't.

twelve: evangeia

It was impossible to say how much true urgency lay behind the mission I had offered Murphy. That we had even found the universe to which he would be sent meant the Selenites could find it as well. It could be years or decades before they moved against that world; they could be doing so already. I gave him two weeks to consider. More would be pointless.

The Selenite incursion against Murphy's Earth had unfolded over centuries. In part, they were slowed by the efforts of my father's folk, but also in part... there had simply been no haste. A billion-year-old multiversal hivemind of humanoid quasiinsects both perceives and moves through time in ways utterly foreign to all other consciousness.

It did not, in any case, matter. In less than a week's time, I had my answer.

"Of course, the primitive accepted your offer," Aelestaire said. "My one surprise in this extends no further than your own uncertainty in that outcome."

My immediate superior among my father's folk had asked for a personal briefing. The time required was easily spared from my various projects, so I consented.

"Murphy has surprised us before," I replied. "He may be more unique than you think."

We were seated at a table on a balcony overlooking a chasm that seemed truly bottomless, one of thousands such balconies ringing that vast space. Somewhat closer above us, the chasm's edge. Above that, the unblinking stars of space. A great well bored into the heart of an airless world.

A grandmaster of The Order had once described such places in what was taken as an imaginary romance. Once the original inhabitants had been driven away, my father's folk had claimed it as their own.

A discrete automaton refilled Aelestaire's glass, then my own. Aelestaire sipped of his wine and shrugged. "A truly unique personality cannot be cultivated in a life measured in mere decades. I grant you, though, this one of your mother's kind has not served us poorly."

"Indeed not," I said. "For all that, his short span has not given him the subtlety to appreciate the contempt in which he is held by those who have sworn their lives to his world's defense."

Aelestaire was entirely of my father's people and had spent most of his own long life cultivating an advanced and unique sense of irony in the place we'd claimed. I can somewhat pass among my mother's people as one among them. Aelestaire could certainly do no such thing had he even wished it. Taller than myself, his long hair was the color of rosetinted silver, his eyes a gray so pale as to be almost white. He was dressed in a black robe shot through with streaks of iridescent crimson. I had myself opted for a formal black tunic and slacks.

It would perhaps amuse Murphy to know that I am as much a double agent as he once was have been one for centuries. The organization in which I hold my true (and modest) rank is even further beyond the 'Order' into which I had inducted Murphy than that order is beyond the company of spies and criminals from which I had inducted him.

For all I know, the nested Russian dolls of secrets containing secrets does not end with me. I have visited the 'Earth' of my father's people. I found it bewildering and incomprehensible. The child of a Roman centurion stationed too long in Gaul would have likely felt much the same upon visiting Rome, as would an Iraqi child of an American officer upon seeing New York City. In all cases, the veiled contempt for the mother's people would remain unremarked and ignored.

"Neither contempt nor condescension is in any way intended, Evangeia," Aelestaire replied. "Your pardon begged if any given."

"Accepted," I said.

"What of your project to find other hybrids?"

Although not so common as the folklore of Murphy's Earth assumes, Selenite hybrids like Case are not rare. Once we had determined the usefulness of Case under the appropriate circumstances, finding others like him, others like Murphy whose minds had been touched by such creatures, became one among our priorities.

"What we have found so far is of little utility," I replied. "Case's abilities were already active when we captured him; the few other active hybrids we have found have no bond with humans remotely approaching Murphy's background or training. I feel our best option remains reproducing this psychic connection using our own technology."

Murphy had guessed correctly that he was not an ideal candidate for this project but had no idea how much less ideal our other options were. Further, he had no idea how much he would be used as a working prototype for something much larger.

Why Selenites had ever chosen to blend with humankind remains an abiding mystery. Certainly, Case had proven useful—but Case was a rarity and an anomaly... somewhat like myself. In the absolute reality of the true multiverse, is there a world where I am the tortured half-human monster and Case the torturer?

If so... it is only just.

"Pursue other options as you see fit," Alestaire said. "But proceed with this plan as well. Grant your vassal the gift of life, send him into this otherworld you have found, place faith in the possibility that he may live up to your hopes... or at least fail in a manner we can learn from."

* * * *

"The last time I freed an angel," Murphy said, "the circumstances were fairly unique. I'm guessing you have something a little bit different in mind this time... am I right?"

I had given him two weeks to decide—an invisibly short span to my father's folk, but my mother's mayfly people make greater use of their shorter lives. Weeks can be eternities to humans in pain. This I know, having inflicted much pain.

The Murphy that returned to us a mere week later was not the man I had sought out on the streets of a human city. He was still a grizzled remnant of the vicious brute I'd once recruited, but something else had changed.

Where he had once been resigned and detached, he now seemed angry and impatient.

Perhaps it was the prospect of returned youth and extended life. The gift of life is seldom offered for the simple reason that it rarely turns out well. My mother's people are evolved to breed and die. That they have themselves extended their lives by mere decades has much to do with their impending self-inflicted extinction. Give their entire species the long lives of my father's folk, and they would be as great a plague upon the cosmos as the Selenites themselves.

We sat in the same conference room where I had briefed Murphy a week before. In the containment dome next to us, final modifications were being carried out on the Case hybrid in preparation for this mission. Soon, modifications would be carried out on Murphy as well.

Were I younger or less of my father's folk... I might actually grieve for him.

"The circumstances of Morningstar's release from Earth were more unique than you can imagine," I told him. "The Dawn Matter shard the Selenites directed to Earth was perhaps the only such thing to be found anywhere in this galaxy."

"Dawn Matter shard?"

"I believe Morningstar referred to it as a 'Seraphim Stone.'"

"It looked like a rock," Murphy said. "If he wanted to call it a 'stone,' I didn't have a problem with that. You want to call it something else? I'm good with that, too."

"Call it whatever you want," I told him. "But understand the scope of what occurred. You befriended a living remnant of the creation of your entire universe. You helped this thing, this 'angel' if you like, evade a trap set by beings themselves not much younger.

"'Unique' merely begins to describe such an event. But we learned from it."

"Like what?"

"We learned enough about how the Seraphim Stone regenerated Morningstar to determine a way to achieve something similar through other means."

"Go on."

"Please understand that no condescension is meant in this," I said. "But explaining this to you is roughly comparable to explaining your cell phone to a Neolithic hunter."

"No offense taken, Evangeia—I don't understand my cell either. But I still know how to use the durned thing. Hopefully, this thingamajig you expect me to deliver is at least as user-friendly."

"More, actually."

thirteen: murphy

The saucer they sent to pick me up the second time was piloted by the same unsmiling woman who'd been at the controls the first time. There was apparently no one else aboard. I didn't feel like making small talk. Fortunately, neither did she.

I was met on arrival by Evangeia, this time dressed in a severe black tunic and slacks. For reasons of my own, I was dressed in black as well. In the same conference room she'd briefed me in before, I received my final mission briefing.

I'd showed up pissed off, and found myself getting more pissed by the minute. I'd always understood that I was a Neanderthal compared to Evangeia's kind, but I didn't particularly appreciate being reminded of it. Being assured that the package I would be delivering matched my cell phone for usability did not reassure me. I actually hate my fucking phone.

I probably shouldn't—I'm as dependent on the damned thing as everyone else is—but I can still remember a time when cradle-to-grave immersion in technology wasn't considered a goddam given. I was about to surrender whatever life I had left to technology I didn't even understand—and I wasn't exactly happy about that, either.

But I knew what my options were... and it didn't seem very likely that I could back out now.

At the end of the conference table, a panel in the wall I'd not noticed before slid up. An object rolled into the middle of the conference table on a conveyor belt I also hadn't noticed, coming to rest between myself and Evangeia.

The object on the table seemed to be three conjoined black metal cubes, perhaps the size of a softball or a grapefruit, each one etched with intricate designs that reminded me of circuitry. Evangeia picked it up, twisted one of the end cubes 90 degrees clockwise, then 180 degrees counterclockwise. The cube came away in her hand. Setting it on the table, she did the same with the remaining two cubes. Then she touched other controls on the separated cubes—which then unfolded before me.

"Color-coded for my convenience," I said, looking into the opened cubes.

"Very much so," Evangeia replied.

Within each opened cube, I could see a golf ball-sized colored metallic sphere—one blue, one red, one green. Like the cubes, they were intricately etched.

"This," Evangeia pointed to the blue sphere, "This will, when activated in the near vicinity of a Dawn Matter entity such as Morningstar, do what you once did—free that entity from Earth. Restore it, that it may return to the cosmos."

"That's what Morningstar wanted," I said. "This archangel or archangel-equivalent may have other plans, may not even be sentient—what Case found could be another Seraphim Stone, for all you know. What then?"

"Then there is this," she said, pointing to the red sphere. "You may recall that Morningstar described himself as a 'conscious singularity.' This is no hyperbole. I am sure that you are aware of another type of singularity commonly described as a 'black hole.'"

"I know they suck. Past that, not so much."

"That is actually sufficient. Activating this device in the near vicinity of the very unique and specialized variety of singularity we call 'dawn matter' will set off a chain reaction resulting in a far more common type of singularity your people's science refers to as a 'quantum black hole.'"

"I'm guessing it would be somewhat detrimental to my health to be in the near vicinity of this 'chain reaction,'"
I said. "Is there a time delay—or is that when this turns into a suicide mission?"

"You are in no danger of being sucked into the event horizon of an angel as it collapses into its own black hole," Evangeia said. "However, the Cherenkov radiation released by such an event would almost certainly be lethal at short range."

I snorted. "A lot more lethal for the 'angel.'"

"That we do not know," she said. "Quite possibly, such a being could survive the experience of falling within their own event horizon. Regardless, the chain reaction is not instantaneous. You will have time to reach a safe distance."

"How much distance qualifies as 'safe'?"

"Twenty meters should be sufficient. More would be better."

"No doubt," I said. "So, what's the last one? Is that how I get home?"

"Yes." She touched the control surfaces on the cubes holding the blue and red spheres. They folded shut. "Pick it up," she said. "Hold it."

I reached into the opened cube. My fingers tingled as I grasped the sphere. Picking it up felt... strange. It didn't feel heavy, but it seemed oddly massive. It resisted being moved. "Interesting," I said.

"At the core of what you hold," Evangeia said. "Is a small quantity of what is perhaps best described as 'pseudo dawn matter.' It is not truly of this universe. It is a remnant of this universe's creation."

"You mean, 'creation by God'?" I said.

"If you believe in such things," Evangeia replied. "All of these devices will send a unique coded signal through the micro-rift when activated, so we can know of your mission's success. This device announces your desire to return. Only activate it if you are in a place where you can safely remain relatively close at hand until we can arrange your retrieval."

"And how long is that likely to take?"

"The… resources required for your transportation are not under my direct control. But I will do everything I can to expedite on your behalf. Weeks, in any event. Months, possibly."

"Years?" I asked.

She shrugged. "It is not impossible."

The oddly massive sphere I held in my hand was also cold to the touch—and stayed that way. Amid the elaborate etchings on the surface, I could see what looked like a pair of concentric circles. I pointed to it. "Is that the activation control?"

"It is. All of these devices activate the same way. You will be shown what to do."

 The object in my hand was not the most alien thing I had ever seen… but it came close. Unlike other tools I'd been given at various times by The Order, it was undisguised in any way. It was fundamentally… alien. "Is this also a radiation hazard?" I asked.

"No," she said. "But I would still not recommend having it on your person when you activate it."

I shuddered and put the thing back in its enclosure. Evangeia touched a control surface. The enclosure folded back into a cube.

"There is one other thing you need to know," she said, "and this is quite important: Until you have need of any of these devices, they must remain in their containment vessels. Even more important: if you are to activate any one of these devices, it is only one—that the other two remain in containment and not in close proximity at the time of activation."

"Define 'important,'" I asked. "What would happen?"

"The pseudo-dawn matter contained in these devices is not truly stable. The activation of any one of them will nullify the containment fields of the others, resulting in a rapid and uncontrolled release of energy."

"That's sounding a lot like a bomb. Just how much 'energy' are we talking about?"

"Small but significant," She replied. "In terms you are familiar with, perhaps as much as several kilotons—but there is no danger so long as you follow your instructions, Murphy."

Just do as you're told, monkey boy, I thought. It'll all be just fine.

Yeah... right.

Evangeia locked the three cubes together again. "It is best," she said, "that the outer containment vessels remain joined. It strengthens the effect and conserves power consumption."

"Is that a concern? If the juice runs out, what then? Does that 'small but significant' energy release just go ahead and happen, anyway?"

She shook her head. "The devices will remain powered for decades, perhaps as long as a century. Long enough for the completion of your mission."

I've been told I have anger management issues, but I don't think so. When I get mad, I've usually got a good reason. As soon as that reason goes away, so does the anger. Not everyone sees it that way, of course—but it works for me.

I've also been told that I make bad decisions out of anger—and that might actually be true. I'd been angrier than I had been in decades when I decided to do this. I wasn't having second thoughts, but the enormity of what I'd agreed to was beginning to sink in.

"That would be a damned sight more reassuring," I said, "were it not for the many other things I am clearly not being told, Evangeia. You aim to send me to another universe with what amounts to a backpack nuke—supposedly in exchange for a rejuvenation treatment that might not even work. You're promising me a ride home—but you're also telling me it might be years before that ride shows up.

"You haven't even told me how I get there in the first place or how long that takes. You've told me I'll be equipped with what I need for this mission—but haven't even come close to explaining what that means. There is a long and growing list of things that I'm sort of taking on faith at this point—all in exchange for a second life, I'll probably just fuck up as bad as I did the first time around.

"Yeah, I know: I might as well be a caveman compared to you, and you are doing me one big damn favor—but it sounds like I'm doing no small favor of my own. 'Need to know' ain't gonna cut it—not this time, Evangeia. Either start leveling with me now—or find yourself another monkey boy."

fourteen: evangeia

I had warned Aelestaire of this, but he would not listen. "The primitive will be besotted with the idea of immortality is likely besotted with yourself as well. Tell it what is required to gain its consent. I see no need for any further."

"And the offer to retrieve him, once this is done?"

He shrugged. "The offer is genuine, but let us be realistic: This mission might require decades, may fail, may be superseded by your plan to recruit others. In any event, the primitive will be among its own kind... and we are, after all, rather doing it a great favor."

"We are sending him into another universe where he will likely die. How is this a favor, Elder?"

Aelestaire gestured for more wine. "I think we do your vassal a great favor, Evangeia. We are extending its sad little life—perhaps greatly—and offering it a chance to live that life on a world its species has yet to destroy. We are even offering—at no small expense—to retrieve it, should it wish to return to its homeworld All we ask in return is that it once again do as you have trained it. All that is being asked of you is that you continue to do as you've sworn and not indulge in absurd sentimentalities—for, after all, it is not as though this were one of our own."

No, it was not.

It never had been... not for centuries.

But it was going to be.

* * * *

I stood from the table and looked at Murphy for a long moment. For all that he had aged, I could still see the 'primitive' who had once sworn loyalty to beings he barely understood.

Who had sworn loyalty to me.

The look in his eyes told me plainly that he knew he was being lied to once again, being manipulated once again. There was more there—pain, anger, resignation. Other things as well, things I could barely understand despite my long centuries... or perhaps could not understand because of them.

I had lied and lied and lied—and the biggest lie was the one learned from my father and told endlessly to myself, the lie that justified all the other lies. My very existence was rooted in that lie. I had been conceived of it. I had sworn my life to it. I suddenly realized I could defend that lie no more.

And even more suddenly, more than I ever would have thought possible, I knew I could do this no more.

Perhaps I am human, after all.

Breaking Murphy's gaze, I looked past him to those I knew watched. A decision I had not even known I was making was now clear in my mind.

"This ends," I said. "This ends now! Offer him the Obligation... or accept the end of mine."

Part 2: The Fortuned and the Obligate

one: murphy

From yet another hillside, I watched what I would've once called 'a craft of The Order' ascend into yet another night sky and streak away. I had different names for things now.

A lot of things.

I'd been here before, more or less. Astoria had been one of the places where I'd discovered how much I loved the Northwest, back when my wife and I were coming up from the Gulf Coast every chance we had and wondering about making a home here. It was also one of the places I could never quite bring myself to visit again after Caroline left me. It just hurt too damned much.

That pain was now literally a universe away, along with everyone and everything else I had ever known or loved. Or had hated, or despised, or been utterly indifferent to.

Everything.

Not for the first time, the sheer magnitude of it took my breath away. What I had thought of as 'loneliness' for so many years now seemed a very small thing. But I had a job to do... that much, at least, was still the same.

The hillside I was on overlooked a little town built on lower and steeper hills that rolled down to a waterfront and a bay-like expanse, the mouth of a massive river. The town was still called 'Astoria,' the river was still called 'Columbia,' the ocean to the west was still the 'Pacific.' If this universe really was branched from mine, it had happened so recently I could pick up a newspaper and read it. I could pick up a history book and skip to the last chapter or two without missing a thing.

Or not... no one really knew.

I began the trek down the hill toward the lights of the town. Those lights were dimmer and more yellow than the last streetlights I'd seen, but they were bright enough. A wind was rising from the west, bringing in fog and rain. Except for the streetlights below and occasional scant moonlight through the gathering clouds, the night was pitch black. The hill was steep and sparsely wooded.

The trail I was on... wasn't much of a trail.

Until recently, I would've done no such thing. But there had been a time in my life when making my way through the dark in strange places had pretty much been my life, in places a lot more dangerous than this. I had advantages now that would've been nice back in the day, doing The Company's dirty deeds.

Not to mention that I felt pretty damned good.

I was wearing heavy hiking boots, jeans, a flannel shirt, and an oilskin duster—not one of which would've been worth a moment's notice or comment in 'my' Astoria. I was also wearing my favorite old leather jacket under the oilskin. Evangeia had made me take off the pins and other decorations, even though I was pretty sure no one around here knew a live Kennedy from a dead one. But it was a good luck charm, as well as a connection to a past that seemed more distant with every passing moment.

I also had a knapsack and a walking stick I wouldn't need once I got to level terrain. These items would've been pretty non-noteworthy as well, back where I came from, except for being pretty 'old school' in outward fabrication and design. The stick was solid wood and heavy, not the featherweight thing I'd used as a cane for the last year or so. The outside of the knapsack was entirely made of leather, canvas, and wool. My boots were also all leather. There were reasons for this.

Walking down a steep hill in the dark and the rain in a world not quite my own, I found myself yet again contemplating the utter improbability of it all.

murphy (inter lunam)

I had been given contact info and two weeks to decide if I was going to use it or not. Actually, staying for the funerals would've run three weeks... so I didn't. People I will never see again in a world I may also never see again probably think a little less of me, but I've gotten kind of used to that. I've been let down a few times as well. In my mind, it sort of balances out.

It hurt to let the old Porsche go, but I damn sure couldn't take it with me. My mechanic found a good home for it. The biggest obstacle to setting everything else in order was convincing my attorney I hadn't succumbed to dementia when I told her what I wanted. Eventually, she decided that my money wasn't senile in any case... and did as I asked.

Roughly a week later, I found myself back at the new and improved Area Fifty Whatever—receiving the last mission briefing I would ever receive in my own world. Questions were answered, and a lot more raised. Par for the course, really. It has been a long time since I had ever taken any of the various people and sort of people I've worked for at their word on much of anything. But I had always given Evangeia credit for at least trying.

That might be why the evasiveness on my supposed ride home and other details annoyed me... or maybe it was the fact that hitching a ride on other transportation was pretty much out of the question. It wasn't that big a deal, really—I'd already been on a one-way trip of a different kind two weeks before, and it sounded like the scenery might be more interesting on this one. But anyone who thought I was going to settle for 'need to know' on this assignment was even crazier than I was for accepting it.

But I finally got my answers.

Holy shit, did I ever get answers.

I was sitting in the same conference room where I'd gotten the Wormhole 101 lecture. Evangeia was sitting across from me, in a severe black tunic that looked more like a uniform than anything I had ever seen her wear. Between us on the table: a small case containing three metallic spheres in bright primary colors, not quite the size of golf balls. Size isn't everything: Even the green one that was supposed to ring up my supposed ride home would do a fair imitation of the much larger sphere Robert Oppenheimer had tested at Trinity... if mishandled.

I was feeling just a bit mishandled myself. I was on the verge of telling Evangeia to take The Job and shove it... and I think she knew it.

Suddenly, she stood and looked at me for a long moment. I had often felt like a mouse saying 'hi' to a cobra looking into those ice-blue eyes, but not this time. Her expression was nothing I had ever seen. Whatever emotion it conveyed was beyond my experience.

Then she looked up from me and stared hard at nothing in particular behind me—other than a blank wall. "This ends," she said. "This ends now. Offer him the Obligation. Or accept the end of mine."

The wall melted away. In the space past where it had been sat one of Evangeia's people—unlike Evangeia herself, a being who could not be mistaken for human under any circumstances, moonlight be damned.

Call him an elf-lord in black armor, if you like, topped off with an iridescent caftan Liberace would've died for. Eight feet tall and spectrally thin, he unfolded from the chair like a praying mantis and walked into the room. Evangeia held his gaze the entire time, even when she had to look up to do so.

Finally, the being spoke—in perfect, unaccented English. "What you ask is not entirely unheard of, perhaps even warranted given the circumstances." He turned and looked at me. The 'mouse saying hi to a cobra' feeling came back in spades. "Mr. Murphy, the mission you had already accepted would very much change your life, as well as extend it. What is being offered now changes it even more in ways you cannot possibly know—but perhaps can learn. Your friend asks much on your behalf... but I will permit it."

He turned back to Evangeia. "This is yours, yours entirely. If there is a cost to be paid, that is yours as well. The way forward passed through Foothold in any case. You may prepare your candidate there."

He walked back to the hidden room he had entered from and turned to look at me once more. "It is only fair to offer you one last chance to pass upon this. There truly is no turning back."

"Thanks," I said. "But I'm good."

"Then I see no need for further delays," he replied.
"We leave within the hour."

The 'wall' melted back into place. Evangeia returned to her seat at the conference table across from me. The odd play of emotion I'd seen earlier was once again hidden behind the demeanor of a sphinx.

"So," I said. "Does 'leave within the hour' spare any time to tell me what, exactly, is going on?"

"In fact, it does not. I ask that the trust you've given me for decades extend to this. I just made a demand on your behalf I should've made on my own—a long, long time ago. Because there is a need for you, that demand was accepted."

Another 'initiation' wasn't exactly what I was looking for at this late stage of my life—but apparently, that's exactly what I was in for. "Sounds like you just moved me to the big kid's table," I said.

"Essentially," she replied.

"And I'm guessing that was one of the adults."

"Very much so."

two: evangeia

When we created Murphy's 'Order,' we largely modeled it upon the various occult groups already in place upon his world. But we had another model as well. For that reason, I knew he could easily be told what was required in order for him to accept the Obligation. I also knew that he could not possibly be told everything.

But precedent permitted this.

Certainly, my father had told me the bare minimum required before accepting mine.

I do not regret that commitment. It has given my life meaning in ways it otherwise would have lacked, as well as offered protection. Over the centuries, I have often needed both. It has provided little in the way of solace or comfort—but I have learned to follow the ways of my father's people, who are largely beyond the need of such things.

But truly being of my father's people... that is another matter entirely.

I do not fully understand why Aelestaire's condescension toward Murphy should have mattered any more than his condescension toward me or why Murphy himself should matter any more than the hundreds other of my mother's people I have used, lied to, and occasionally rewarded over centuries. Even less do I understand why I offered to give up, on his behalf, an Obligation from which I have derived so much.

I do understand why Aelestaire consented. There was simply too much at stake for him to have done otherwise.

Within the bounds of what I was free to say, I tried my best to prepare Murphy in the short time he had left in his own world. "'Foothold' is the original colony of my people in your Earth's universe," I told him. "It is quite old, very little like anything else you have ever seen."

"Is it a long trip?" he asked. We were in an outbuilding on the rock shelf overlooking the base, surrounded by craft of my father's people. Shortly, we would be boarding one.

"Not at all," I told him. "It is the facility on the far side of Earth's moon, of which you have known for years."

"Not by that name."

"You will be learning new names for many things, Murphy."

"Yeah, I reckon so—is that where I get juiced?"

"If you are referring to the rejuvenation treatment, yes. All preparation for your mission will occur at Foothold. Then you will be taken to the rift leading to the universe where your mission occurs."

"Which is on Earth?"

"No. It is in fairly deep space, which we think may be among the reasons we have found no evidence on this other Earth of Selenites."

Murphy sighed and shuddered. "This just gets bigger and bigger, boss. I sometimes have a hard time wrapping my mind around it."

"You have dealt with much strangeness in your life, Murphy, and no small danger. I have confidence in you. And I will personally see to it that you have everything you need for this."

"Seems you've already taken a personal stake in this—which I did not expect and for which I thank you. Your boss didn't seem too happy about the deal you just backed him into offering me... whatever the hell that is."

It was oddly affecting to be offered Murphy's gratitude. Aelestaire might have considered the simple dignity with which it was offered 'primitive.' I did not.

"Aelestaire is as committed to this mission as any of us and has been Obligated far longer than either you or I have lived. This is far from the first time he and I have disagreed. And he can be gracious—after all, you and I shall be guests in his home while you are prepared for your mission."

"First I'd heard of it," Murphy grumbled. "I'll believe the 'gracious' part when I see it."

"There has not been time to tell you everything, and for that, I apologize. But that shall change."

three: murphy

By the time I got into town, the fog had thickened, and the rain was a steady drizzle. The oilskin had a hood; I flipped it up. I would shortly be finding out just how good the gear and supplies I'd been given for this mission really were—not the angel-dispatching stuff, the other stuff.

The fact that I was in another universe was beginning to sink in in various ways. The hill I'd been landed on is best known in 'my' Astoria for a tower monument with a lovely view and one scary damned spiral staircase. Here, a lighthouse had taken the place of the Astoria Column. I'm guessing the staircase was pretty much the same.

Perhaps the biggest difference: no bridge.

The Astoria-Megler bridge across the mouth of the Columbia is reasonably famous in my Earth's Northwest. In this version, it had never been built. The crossing was still by way of one of the scarier ferry rides in North America, across a body of water that was probably called 'the graveyard of the Pacific' here as well.

I was shortly either going to be checking into a cheap hotel for the evening or winding up in jail. The jail in question had been turned into a film museum where I was from, but the consequence of passing fake money was largely the same in either universe. As long as there was a warm, dry bed involved, I was good either way... my 'jail cherry' got popped a long time ago, and it had been one helluva long day.

One helluva long ride, for that matter.

murphy (inter lunam)

There's not much I can say about the experience of flying to the moon in a flying saucer that George Adamski hasn't already covered pretty well. The inflight service sucks, but at least it's a short trip. By the time we arrived, a feeling of strangeness had set in... and has pretty much been with me ever since.

64

I had always known that Evangeia was part space alien, had always been short on the details, had always known better than to ask. I eventually knew that 'space alien' wasn't really right, but it was useful shorthand in my mind for something a lot more complicated.

Now that I was surrounded by them, I was going to have to stop using mental shorthand.

Foothold is just that: A reclaimed Selenite colony that Evangeia's people had taken when they first got here and kept. That didn't keep the little grey bastards from slipping in for the occasional cattle mutilation or anal probing, but they'd been served notice that claiming my world outright wasn't going to happen—not if Evangeia's folks had anything to say about it.

The reclaimed colony is an enormous pit that looks from the outside like any other lunar crater and goes deep into the Moon itself. Just how deep is something I'm not clear on. I know that the upper levels are considered choice real estate, the lower levels not so much. Evangeia's people are not capitalists or communists or anything else that translates easily into baseline Earth human terms. But they do have a hierarchy, which apparently has a lot to do with the fact that they are some very long-lived bastards and willing to wait for their piece of the pie.

Evangeia's boss had been working on his piece for a few thousand years. It was a nice piece.

I didn't see that much of Aelestaire d'Aigremont's home. I mostly stayed in the guest wing that had been equipped with earth-normal gravity. Even that was pretty lavish to a country boy like me. There were high ceilings by necessity, soft lighting from sources difficult to spot, furniture crafted from materials that could have been anything for all I knew, but it was comfortable and largely analogous to what might be found in the home of any obscenely wealthy human being.

The part I stayed in had obviously been furnished to make someone like me feel as comfortable and at home as possible, seemingly confirming rumors I'd heard over the years as to who the Grandmasters of The Order—not to mention a few politicians—really worked for. During my treatment and training, I would be staying in a bedroom adjacent to a large sitting room equipped with a balcony, complete with a kitchen and a small but well-stocked bar. I was free to go elsewhere but advised not to.

"You are a guest, not a prisoner," Evangeia told me. "But you are a guest in a home built and maintained to meet the needs of a culture many tens of thousands of years older than your own. I do not and will not condescend to you, Murphy. But your impetuousness very much needs to be curbed in this place. Aelestaire has consented to your rejuvenation. Resurrecting you as well is likely beyond his generosity."

I pretty much doubted the existence of a single generous bone in Aelestaire's entire skinny body. I later learned that the 'armor' I'd glimpsed under his robes was an exoskeleton he'd find Earth-level gravity difficult without. That would be about the only thing I'd gotten wrong from my first impression. As far as he was concerned, I was a somewhat useful monkey boy who was being rewarded far more than he deserved. I'd seen that look before.

We were sitting in the lounge of the One Gee guest wing. I'd been tempted by the balcony, but the low gravity and view of an apparently bottomless pit were too much for me. A beer would've been nice, but so was the wine I'd found. "I think it's time for the rest of the story, Evangeia. I can't back out now. It would be nice to know how long I'm going to be here and what the preparation for this mission consists of."

Evangeia sat across from me with a wine glass of her own. Behind her, I could see the lighted balconies on the far side of Foothold, as well as flitting things in the space between that I suspected were Evangeia's people playing 'Batman' in the low gravity. You'd think the setting would make her seem more unearthly than ever. Instead, she seemed more human.

"The preparation consists of the rejuvenation therapy to which you've already consented, as well as some minor surgical implants, as well as a brief education on the responsibilities you will be accepting. You will also receive briefings on your destination. Our timeline is still to have you on your mission within two weeks."

"I don't recall a previous discussion on the subject of 'implants,'" I told her.

"It was implied. They are necessary for the communication link to the Case Hybrid and have other uses as well. You were going to receive a limited version specific for this mission. That is no longer the case."

"Because...?"

"Because you are now a candidate to join the same organization of which I am a member, the same organization you've actually served ever since you joined The Order. This is what I threatened to resign from in order to obtain it for you."

She sipped more wine. "Aelestaire's promise to retrieve you at the end of your mission was not false, but it would have been fulfilled at his convenience. If you accept the same Obligation that he and I have both accepted, you become one of us. The Obligation goes both ways."

"And just what is that 'Obligation'?"

"I will educate you. It is not simple."

four: evangeia

In their own language, my father's folk call themselves 'The Fortuned.'

This naming starts from a simple truth: We have, indeed, been more fortunate than any other humanoid species we've encountered in the multiverse—we evolved earlier and better; found ways to further leverage our good fortune.

But it encompasses more than that. Long before we found and explored actual rifts between worlds, we had theorized about the true scope of the multiverse. If absolute reality is the infinitely dimensioned matrix of everything that ever has, will, or could be, then what accounts for any one path taken above any other? Was our good fortune merely the sum total of several million years of 'luck'... or something more?

Over time, The Fortuned came increasingly to believe that their good fortune was intrinsic to the design of the greater cosmos—not 'intended' by gods we no longer believed in, but no less predestined.

Then came the Selenites—the Greys. The infesters and destroyers of worlds.

The Obligate is neither priesthood, military order, occult fraternity, or an interdimensional police force... but it has functioned as all of these things and more.

In simplest terms, there are those among the Fortuned who feel their collective good fortune carries with it an obligation. That obligation begins with a fundamental resistance to the implacable enemy that threatened to end our good fortune. The folklore of Murphy's Earth is as likely to cast little grey aliens as benevolent as not. They will never know that they can thank the Obligate for that ambiguity.

I had taken the Obligation from my own father when I was barely more than a child. Had I known then what I know now, I might well have refused. My father enlisted me in a war that had lasted for millennia. He did so with the best of intentions: the desire to ensure that the half-breed child he'd fathered would be acknowledged and accepted among his own kind, knowing full well the likelihood that I would not always be under his protection.

What my father could not know, was essentially blind to, was that he could only force my acknowledgment... not my acceptance. The Fortuned believe in very little as they believe in their own Fortune. But even those like Aelestaire who would lay down their lives in the Obligation they've taken to defend the less fortuned... see little need to share fortune of their own.

And so I have spent thousands of years of my own life fighting a war I inherited from my father's people, defending my mother's people from a variety of threats—even while permitting the threat they pose to themselves. And so I have lied to my mother's people and used them to suit my father's ends, and caused far too many among my mother's people to give up their sad, short lives to causes they would not understand... were I even free to tell them.

But after a thousand years, I finally had to say: enough.

I told Murphy as much of this as I could. The Obligation is seldom offered outside The Fortuned. When it is, the candidate must be informed, as much as possible, of the true nature of what is offered and what is expected in return. But not all secrets can, or should, be shared.

I had little delusion over the likely outcome of the mission Murphy had accepted. The highest probability was that he would die in a world not quite his own, accomplishing nothing. I was already making plans for that outcome, as was my duty. But he was going to die anyway... as do all my mother's people.

But there was also a more than trivial chance he might succeed. Were that to happen and he wished to return to us, I was going to see to it that he had that opportunity. What might happen past that was impossible to say. In his own small way, Murphy had led a 'fortuned' life. Should he choose to continue it in the service of The Obligate, he was welcome to do so.

Murphy had an advantage over me when I had been in his place: he had spent most of his life fighting a variety of secret proxy wars in various ways, including mine. Far more than I had, he knew what he was getting into. For all his haughty arrogance, Aelestaire d'Aigremont did not truly know what he was getting in return with his new Obligate candidate.

But like all of my various peoples... both my master and my protégé were willing to take a chance.

And so was I.

five: murphy

The hotel I checked into had a different name and a different clientèle back where I'm from. This version of Astoria had a lot less tourist trade; a lot more logging and fishing business. There was still a bar in the basement with a heavily local tap list but no rooftop deck and no boutique decor. The fabricated currency I'd paid with had been accepted without comment, as well it should—anyone who wanted to do a metallurgical analysis would find far more gold and silver than the stuff it was made to imitate.

I'd pretty much given up on understanding Fortuned technology. I knew that the survey ship that brought me here had saturated this world with microscopic drones on its first visit that by the time the ship returned with me, enough data had been acquired to fabricate things like local money. Within reason, I had the means to make more.

The bed was comfortable and warm. There was a television in the room, but if I wanted to watch it, I would have to give up some more of my better-than-real fake coins to check out a handful of local channels. There was a washstand and a toilet in my room. If I wanted to take a shower, I was going to need to go down the hall. I was also going to need to take some of my fake coins with me.

The mission protocol called for me to do a systems check on my implants as soon as possible—but the people who had drafted that plan weren't in a position to do much about it if I had other priorities. Either the shit worked, or it didn't. If it didn't, my revised plans for the next day were going to start with a quick scan of the 'help wanted' classifieds in the Daily Astorian. I couldn't exactly live on fairy gold for the rest of my life.

But I could certainly afford a drink or two.

The elevator to the basement was the same as it was in another version of this building—but less old-fashioned here and also in better repair. I'd stashed my gear in the room. I wasn't particularly worried about hotel theft aborting my mission. It might've looked like an old canvas rucksack, but the technology did not exist in this world for anyone other than myself to either move it or open it. And—even though I'd been 'asleep' for most of that time—I hadn't had a damn beer in months.

The bar was comfortably dim, with heavy wood paneling and leather upholstery. The bartender was probably close to my real age—heavyset, with thinning, slicked-back hair and thick glasses. There were few customers. A middle-aged couple in matching plaid mackinaws sat at a table, a guy in a watch cap and a peacoat was camped out at the end of the bar. In a back booth, a younger couple were paying more attention to each other than their drinks and would likely be soon leaving.

"What's good for an IPA?" I asked the bartender.

"Seadog's good."

"Let's have a pint—anyone reading this?" I pointed to a used newspaper next to the cash register.

The bartender shrugged as he drew my pint. "Yesterday's paper."

"Still news to me, brother." Grabbing the paper and the beer, I retired to a booth.

The sports page was almost comprehensible. Rugby and hockey were nothing new, with rugby apparently taking the place of U.S. rules football... but I had no damned idea what 'pelota' was, much less why anyone would give a damn. The political news made no sense whatever... except for the part about the U.S. 'Ambassador' being heckled by protesters upon arrival in San Francisco. The coins I'd used to pay for my room, had they been real, would've been issued by the 'Pacific and Northwest Federation, Bank of Oregon.' At some point, I'd know exactly what that meant.

But I already had a pretty good idea.

I read through the rest of the paper while I sipped my beer. A recent election in the U.S. had apparently turned out about the same as a less recent one in my version of 'America.' Even though the idiot that got elected didn't have quite the same name, he apparently had the same shady connections and bad intentions, not to mention the same reckless tendencies and fondness for online petty insults. At least in this world, he wasn't a problem west of the Mississippi River.

At least not for now.

There were also stories that reminded me one hell of a lot of stuff I used to get paid to write. It might be a coincidence, it might not—I wasn't going to assume anything until I knew a lot more.

The beer was good—not great, but definitely a Northwest-style IPA. Ads in the paper for cannabis products further showed that the 'Oregon' I'd wound up in had a fair amount in common with the one I'd left. One more beer,
I decided that I would pack it in for the evening. Even though I was more caught up on sleep than I had ever been in my entire life, a real bed was sounding better by the minute.

murphy (inter lunam)

"So...this is it?" I said.

A 'day' had passed since I'd arrived on the moon, most of which I had spent sleeping, followed by the first of several briefings by Evangeia on just what I'd gotten myself into. There is an old saying in The Order that 'a true initiation never ends.' I was beginning to realize more than ever just what that meant.

Sitting before me was a small crystal bottle with a matching stopper. The fluid within was a deep amber color, like a good tawny port, but with interesting and complex highlights.

The 'juice.' Elixir vitae. The new life I'd decided to gamble on.

"It is just the beginning," Evangeia said. "But it is an irreversible first step. Take this, and you have agreed to both the extension of your life and committing that life to the mission that brought you here."

"And this means also that I've accepted The Obligation?"

"No, that is different." Evangeia had traded in the severe tunic she'd worn briefing me on Earth for a caftan-like robe not too different from the one her boss had been wearing. I was wearing a gray 'flight suit' that George Adamski would've recognized on the spot. I'd been promised I'd get my old clothes back, as well as some sort of instruction of when it was appropriate to wear what.

"The rejuvenation is offered in exchange for accepting the mission, which you have already done," Evangeia continued. "You could proceed on those terms alone if you preferred."

I shook my head. "I wouldn't be here if I didn't trust you, Evangeia, whether that's a good idea or not. You just tell me what I need to do."

"I am uncertain I deserve such faith, but I will do my best to ensure it is not misplaced. First, drink the elixir.

"Follow-up treatments over the next few days will complete the rejuvenation process, which should be well underway by the time we send you on. You will also undergo a minor surgical procedure once you have either accepted or declined the Obligation. If you accept, you will receive enhancements no different from those I have had for... a long time."

"Assuming this stuff doesn't just kill me, right?"

"While you were sleeping, we conducted a fairly thorough scan, including a check for genetic compatibility issues—necessary to fabricate a serum specific to your genotype. There is no evidence that your body will reject the serum. It remains unknown how long you will live."

"That's been true since the day I was born." I uncapped the bottle, took a taste… then drank it on down.

Hell, it even tasted like a good port. "That would pair well with a decent Stilton."

"We have some if you like. You should definitely have some breakfast."

* * * *

The following days consisted mostly of medical treatments and physical therapy, intermixed with lessons on the history of my hosts and briefings on the world where I might wind up living out the rest of my life. Evangeia was as good as her word on the 'elixir.' Within a day, the chronic hip pain that had troubled me for over a year went away.

Occasionally, Aelestaire would show up to see firsthand how I was progressing, impassive within his exoskeleton. I still felt like a lab animal under that opaque gaze, but I soon realized that everyone else dealing with him felt exactly the same way. Early in my career in The Company, I'd once had the dubious pleasure of meeting George H. W. Bush, and it had pretty much gone the same way. They were both privileged and condescending pricks. At least, so far as I knew, Aelestaire had not inflicted upon the multiverse any idiot children in executive positions.

Whether by way of constant exposure to them, the history lessons, or the gunk rewriting my DNA, Evangeia's people seemed less alien to me with every passing day. Even more, it became difficult to recall why I'd once thought Evangeia herself utterly inhuman.

It might've just been the contrast. Even the Fortuned, who had not adapted to lunar gravity, towered over me while Evangeia topped me by mere inches. And while she was pale by most human standards, the Fortuned were all but albino.

I found myself wondering as well about the commitment she had made all those centuries ago that she had volunteered me to make as well. Oh, I planned to accept. As near as I could tell, it was the same deal I'd accepted from The Order, just with better benefits—and a few added obligations that may or may not matter, depending on whether or not I ever returned. But I had to wonder what it was like to be under such an obligation over centuries.

Maybe I'd even find out.

The briefings on my destination were interesting—either too much or too little information. Had it not been for the work Evangeia was doing with what was left of Colvin Case, this crosstime world might've remained unknown for centuries. The one natural portal to it that had been detected was far out into the Oort Cloud, far from any part of the solar system frequented by any known crosstime-capable species. The prevailing theory was that this, more than anything else, was why this world was apparently undiscovered by Selenites.

There had been one survey trip by a deep-space craft of the Fortuned. The same craft would return to insert me. There would be no further contact until I had finished my mission—one way or another—or someone else was sent to succeed where I'd failed. That one survey trip had accomplished a lot. The Fortuned had been exploring worlds for a long time and had the means to quickly pick up a lot of raw data. But turning that raw data into usable information was going to require the efforts of a trained analyst on the ground.

Me, basically.

Even though the big picture of where this world fit into the multiverse at large remained to be filled in, enough operational data had been acquired that I could be dropped in undetected, equipped to live off the land and execute my mission—kind of like the good old/bad old days doing The Company's underhanded work in Central America, except that this mission seemed a lot more honest.

At least this time around, I actually knew that I was working for a pack of inhuman bastards.

* * * *

Finally, I was as prepped as I was going to be, and it was time for a decision. Once I consented to the Obligation, a surprisingly brief surgical procedure equipped me with the implants I'd been told to expect. I was awake for the procedure. It was nothing compared to getting my wisdom teeth pulled, although a lot more like getting checked for glaucoma.

Later that same 'evening,' Evangeia found me in the lounge of the earth-gravity guest quarters, trying to make sense of the operator's manual for my new hardware. "Leave that," she said. "If you do not mind lunar gravity, there is something I'd like to show you." She was dressed in a longsleeved black gown streaked with silver, her hair once again in a long braid. Not for the first time, I thought about the small fortune she could've made as a fashion model had she ever gotten tired of running the Illuminati.

I was wearing one of the same gray jumpsuits I'd been wearing since I'd arrived. I was looking forward to wearing real clothes again—even if it meant having to go to another universe. "I always RTFM," I replied. "But sure."

She led me to an elevator at the end of the corridor, which took us upward rapidly. When we exited, ahead I saw stars. "We arrived here in what amounts to the lunar night. The sun will be rising shortly. I thought you might wish to see it."

"Mighty kind of you," I said. "Thanks."

She led me to a long, low seat that spanned the width of the window in front of it and sat next to me.

"You need not answer if you do not want," she said. "But before you embark on this mission you've accepted, I should like to ask a question."

"You're entitled to that. What would you like to know?"

She looked straight ahead into the stars for a long moment, then spoke. "I do not believe you consented to this merely for the promise of long life. When the mission was offered, I truly felt you would decline. Less than a week later, you accepted. May I ask why?"

It was my turn for a long pause. "I honestly don't know if I was going to accept or not. After everything I've done over the years, the idea of hanging out in a commune of other old fucks and eventually passing away in my sleep didn't seem like such a bad idea.

"Then I got back to Portland... and found out the other old fucks were already gone."

I wasn't sure how much of this I could explain to Evangeia, for all of her centuries of experience.

"One of my roommates, Gavin, had a couple of bad habits—he liked rough trade, and he liked 'em young.

"Apparently, he made a bad judgment call while I was out of town finding out about this 'mission.' He brought home this one young fella who turned out to have some serious drug issues, who decided that a housing co-op full of comfortably middle-class old people looked like a good score.

"Only it didn't turn out that way.

"He didn't shoot all of my friends, just most of them. He'll never stand trial—he saved the last bullet for himself. If I had been there, I might have made a difference... but I doubt it. I probably would've just gotten shot first."

"I am sorry, Murphy."

"Yeah, me too. I particularly feel bad about not hanging around for the funerals, but that would've cut into your deadline."

"You should have let us know."

"I appreciate that thought, Evangeia. I will go so far as to say I even believe it of you. But your boss doesn't give two shits in a rusty bucket about my personal affairs—and two weeks ago, I would not have believed you much different. Also, I didn't want to stay. I'm long past the point where life stops giving and starts taking. The thought of actually doing something useful again is what decided me. If I get a few more decades in the bargain, that's awesome... but that's not what this is about."

"I see," she said.

Maybe she did, maybe not. "And I have a question for you," I said.

"Ask."

"Why did you intercede on my behalf with Aelestaire? What difference does it make to you whether I get sent on this mission as an agent of The

Order, a member of The Obligate, or some other damn thing you could've cooked up on the spot for my consumption? You don't really have to tell me... but I would like to know."

She sighed. "There are perhaps a thousand reasons, Murphy; perhaps none. I did it in part to better ensure your return—whatever doubts you may have, I do not think it unlikely you will succeed—but I had other reasons as well. You know that I have lived a long, long life, for all that I am half-human."

"Yeah, I know."

"What you cannot know is what that is like. To live among and superficially be accepted by what you think of as 'your kind'... even though you know that thought is never returned."

I had known her for over 30 years, during which time I had never once thought of her as human, had always known she was at least partly something else... never once to give a single thought to feelings I had never been entirely sure she even had.

"I might know more than you think," I said. "You know my full name, right?"

"I know that you prefer simply to be called 'Murphy,' and so I have respected you and done so."

I laughed. "There's reasons for that. My full name is Miguel Alejandro Estefan Murphy—'Mike' to a lot of people; 'Tex,' if you feel like getting your ass kicked. I was named for my Mamacita's three favorite uncles. I grew up on the Northside of Houston, then moved to a slightly better neighborhood with my folks after the Moody Park Riots. I know that none of this means a damn thing to you, but I spent a lot of years growing up getting into just as many fights over getting called a 'gringo' as I did over getting called a 'spic.' Nothing compared to what you've been through, I'm sure... but I just might be able to relate."

She turned to look at me. Her blue eyes were wide in the darkness, softened by a sadness I had never seen. "Once again, I have given you too little credit, Murphy. Tell me... what was your mother's name?"

"Her name was Beatriz. Beatriz Elena Castillo Murphy."

"My mother's name was Evaine. A thousand years ago, she loved a man from another world, had a child, loved her as well—and was then gone in what now seems an instant. Life takes from us all, Murphy. But we give back to others as best we can." She took my hand and held it. "Let us not talk for now. Let us sit and watch the sunrise. It is not like sunrise on Earth. It happens swiftly, then is over."

I did as I was told. She was right.

six: evangeia

We could prepare him no further in any meaningful way. It was time.

Aelestaire would accept Murphy's Obligation. He would then be sent to fulfill it.

Murphy and I were both dressed in the formal black tunics that only the Obligate wear among the Fortuned. We were sitting in the lounge of the guest quarters that had been Murphy's home for the previous weeks. I wanted to make sure he knew what would be expected of him in the ceremony; he wanted a glass of wine.

In truth, I wanted one as well.

"Be certain your implant is active and set to translate, Murphy. It was one thing to get Aelestaire to agree to accept your Obligation. He will certainly not deign to do so in your language."

"From what I know, you could induct me as easily as he could, skip this ceremony, and send me on my way." Murphy tugged irritably at his collar, which I suspected he would rip open the moment he could.

"You will be on your way soon enough and perhaps glad of this one last ceremonial delay. And you know perfectly well why it is Aelestaire doing this and not me. Drink your wine and let your collar be."

"Yes, ma'am."

"All of your belongings and gear have already been stored on the vessel taking you to the rift. We shall prepare you for hibernation, then take you aboard as well."

"I'm still not too crazy about that part—are you sure I can't find a way to make myself useful on the trip out?"

The rift that would take Murphy to his target was deep in space. The journey outward to the Oort Cloud, transition, and journey back to an alternative Earth would take many weeks. It made no sense to not deliver him in stasis.

"I am certain," I told him. "that you would find it quite tedious. And time you are asleep can be used to further train you. You will awaken with skills and knowledge you do not presently have."

"Whoa, you mean I'll know kung fu?"

"Murphy... you already 'know kung fu.'"

* * * *

82

The ceremony went as well as could be expected. To my surprise, Aelestaire opted to dress formally as well for what I was sure he took as a pointless obligation, one that I felt sure would require every persuasive power I had to make sure he would keep.

Then it was over. In every way, I had made Murphy as much one of 'us' as was possible. It wasn't enough, but it would have to do.

To my further surprise, Aelestaire chose to accompany me as I escorted Murphy to the medical facility, where he would soon close his eyes to the only universe he had ever known, and discreetly dropped back as I bade Murphy goodbye.

"I guess this is it, boss."

"Indeed it is, but I am no longer your 'boss.' The Obligation you have accepted supersedes your commitment to The Order. I am simply your colleague... as well as your friend."

"And that is perhaps the strangest thing of all." He took my hands, then embraced me. "Farewell, friend."

Then he released me and turned to Aelestaire, bowing after the manner of my mother's kind. "I'm grateful for this opportunity, promise that the Obligation I've accepted will be fulfilled. Thank you for your hospitality— you have a fine home, sir. It has been an honor." It was strange to hear Murphy speaking the language of my father's people, stranger still to hear Aelestaire respond... in English.

"The honor has been entirely mine, Mr. Murphy. I have every confidence that you shall fulfill The Obligation with distinction. As much as it is possible... may Fortune favor you."

Part 3: Encounter at Corona

It was time to take stock of my situation... and determine how best to proceed.

I had arrived in a new universe and found it not very different from my own. They could've inserted me anywhere in this world. The decision to drop me into the analog of the region I'd called home for over twenty years had been made with a reason. The idea was to keep my disorientation to a minimum, the better to move me forward with my mission.

It was time to put that theory to the test.

I had awakened from a long and deep slumber, though not nearly so long or deep as the one that had brought me here. My dreams had been phantasmagoric recombinations of various parts of my past—which is phantasmagoric enough in the first place. A gray morning light filtered into the window through the fog and the rain.

In addition to a washstand and a toilet, my room included a full-length mirror mounted on the closet door. I stood before it, considered my naked reflection.

Not too bad, all things considered.

My muscle tone was returning, the salt and pepper beard I'd had for years was definitely tending back toward the 'pepper' end of the spectrum. The scalp I'd shaved mostly to avoid embarrassment was once again something I would either need to shave for real or let grow out... a decision I could postpone in either case. My eyes were the same gray I'd been born with, but something seemed different somehow. I'd been promised 'cosmetic' changes. I'd soon know what that meant.

On my left arm, a new tattoo. I'm on the short list of guys I knew from the old punk scene who had not gotten inked all to hell. My little mamacita thought that tats would make me look like a thug, asked that I not get them—and I loved my little mamacita. But she was long gone now... and this was no mere tattoo.

The design was like unto a Tibetan mandala but also like a schematic for an integrated circuit. It marked me as a member of The Obligate. This could be useful in some circumstances, get me killed in others. But unlike the tattoos I'd declined over the years, it marked a decision and an allegiance. Evangeia had one as well... although I had not known that for many decades.

They had not lied; I was feeling younger by the day and looking younger by the week. At the rate things were going, I could start throwing people out of clubs again fairly soon... assuming I had no other options.

'Other options' were both preferred and why I was here. Time to test the hardware.

The implants I'd received included a number of features, but most importantly, they would receive the psychic transmission being sent through a microscopic wormhole somewhere in Greenland... and enable the mutated remains of my former boss to 'paint' the location of the thing I'd come here to find on a heads-up display embedded in my eyes.

I knew the hardware worked. It had been tested before I'd left. Getting the language options set to something I could recognize had been a ton of fun, but I'd otherwise had no problems. It was time to find out if everything still worked as planned on this side of the wormhole.

I sat on my bed and touched a contact surface beneath the skin behind my right ear. While the circuit was closed, I said aloud: "Activate."

The heads-up display jumped into view, overlaying my ordinary vision. Most of the display was taken up by a 3D wireframe of the world I was on. A blinking dot showed my own location in the upper left corner of North America. There was supposed to be another dot showing my target.

It was not to be found.

Something else was blinking, though. Across the bottom of the display, there was a menu of additional options. An option I'd not seen before was blinking insistently. The label read 'SOCIAL INTERFACE.' Since the main reason I even had this gear wasn't working, I touched the contact again and said: "Activate social interface."

The entire display dissolved momentarily into static, then cleared up. The wireframe and menu had disappeared. Something else had changed as well. Colvin Case was sitting in the chair at the room's far end, beneath the pay-per-view TV.

"Hi, old buddy," he said. "I was beginning to wonder how soon you were going to check in."

two: evangeia

The survey craft rose from the docks to head outward. Unlike the sleek vehicles Murphy's people have named 'flying saucers,' this was a deep space vessel: A bulky, brick-like mass of components with a drive on one end and a flight deck on the other. But it was fast, if ungainly. Once it had cleared the docks, it shrank to a pinpoint in less than a second.

"I was wrong," Aelestaire said.

"I crave pardon?" We were in an observation lounge of Foothold's spaceport. I would soon be returning to my duties on Earth.

"I was wrong. I had permitted myself the luxury of condescending to those I'm obligated to defend... and whom I ultimately serve. Your Murphy is a remarkable man—not least for having made me see that."

"Hardly 'my' Murphy."

Aelestaire smiled. "Well, he is ours now in any event, shall be treated as such. I take it you were unable to improve upon his communications equipment?"

"No." The facility in Greenland tapped power directly from the earth's core. We could punch signals through the micro-rift that Murphy's implants would detect. With the exception of the pseudo-dawn matter devices he carried, nothing on the world to which we'd sent Murphy had the power to send anything back.

"A pity we were not able to make greater use of his link with the hybrid."

"The psychic link is unreliable, the hybrid itself more so. It has lied to us before. We are using it to the full extent it can be trusted. For better or worse, Murphy cannot directly communicate with us once he has crossed the rift."

"It is certainly for the worse," Aelestaire replied. "Perhaps the survey craft will return with what we need. Determining the shape and ultimate fate of the multiverse is an excess of responsibility for any man—even one so remarkable as your Murphy."

"He is not 'my' Murphy."

Aelestaire sighed. "Have it as you will."

* * * *

It was a simple question, one all sentients had asked since they first became such.

What shape is the world?

Or, in our case, the true cosmos... the multiverse.

For many centuries, my father's folk and their allies had known a large but finite number of mapped parallel realities—a branching structure in probability space resembling a tree or a river delta, with distinct and known points of divergence between those 'branches'—known points where rifts in the fabric of spacetime made it possible to journey from one to another.

This stable structure had enabled a stable polity among the species aware of it, an alliance led by the Fortuned that largely contained the one species we could not make allies. What greater multiverse the Selenites might know of, we could not say—they do not share knowledge with those they prey upon.

Now there was a multiplicity of such branches, more being detected constantly. The universe to which Murphy had been dispatched to 'hunt angels' was either an incredibly recent divergence from Murphy's own timeline or something even more unheard of: An utterly disconnected, yet highly similar, continuum.

We had to know which.

A recent divergence meant this was merely one among a finite number of accessible earths in parallel universes. Even if that number grew, it meant that the multiverse was an orderly cosmos... one that could be controlled. Even if the alliance led by the Fortuned grew, it could be maintained. The Selenites would remain contained, the balance of power not greatly shifted.

The alternative meant utter chaos.

three: murphy

"I'm gonna guess that you kinda 'get' that I don't really want to talk to you... right?"

A 3D ghost image of my one-time boss and former friend was 'sitting' in a guest chair in the hotel room I'd checked into upon my arrival in a parallel universe. I'd been told that the residual psychic bond from a time he'd essentially tortured me would be used as a means to guide me to my target in this world.

But no one had said anything about talking to the son of a bitch.

In my mind, I heard a dry chuckle I knew very well. "I can see your point, but give me a chance—it's been almost twenty years, after all. And as you may recall, I've suffered a bit as well."

He had a point. The last time I'd actually seen Colvin Case, he had been strung up in the middle of a medical containment facility in a remote part of Greenland, wired into a multitude of machines... including the machinery that enabled him to talk to me now. He was also in the process of visibly mutating physically into what he had always been: a Grey alien/human hybrid.

"You have," I told him, "and you have a point—and I gotta say, you're looking a lot better."

He was. The avatar sitting in a chair in my hotel room was not the misshapen thing I had seen shortly before leaving my Earth, or even the spare, humorless bureaucrat who'd eventually become my boss. This was the Colvin Case who had joined The Company's Central America division some ten years after I had, who not infrequently joined up with me after work to exploit my contacts in Houston's underground club and drug culture... a beefy, blond, friendly kid who was good with computers and good at schmoozing his way up the ladder, but would've lasted maybe a minute in the field. He was even dressed the part, in Cavaricci jeans and a neon-hued Hawai'ian shirt, the hair he hadn't really had for decades liberally moussed and topped off with Ray-Ban Aviators.

"Why should you be the only one who gets to be young again?" said the ghost of my former friend.

"Fair enough," I replied. "I'd sort of been promised I wasn't going to have to talk to you, but if that's what it takes, I can deal. How'd you manage it?"

Case chuckled again. "Your girlfriend and her buddies are not nearly so all-knowing as you've been led to believe. The assumption that they can better control technology I was engineered into existence to use is a typically arrogant conceit."

"Evangeia is hardly my girlfriend. Are the Fortuned a pack of arrogant pricks? Pretty much—they are more or less human, though... which is more than can be said for the folks you threw in with."

"I didn't 'thrown in with' anyone, old buddy—I'm what someone made me. At least you were offered a choice."

"Again, fair enough. But I'm here to do a job, and I need your help to do it. And if you aren't going to help me, I might as well go ahead and hit the 'recall' button."

"I didn't say I wouldn't help," the Case avatar replied. He got out of the chair and 'walked' over to my knapsack. "But if you're talking about activating one of the devices in this bag, I heartily recommend against it."

How he could see the bag was an interesting question. How he knew anything about what was in it was even more interesting... but first things first. "Why so?"

"Because I'm not so sure they do exactly what you think they do. I'm also pretty sure that if you request recall before completing your mission, you may wind up waiting awhile for that ride."

Checking out the 'help wanted' listings for dock work was sounding better by the minute.

"Then what do you suggest?" I asked.

"Stick with the plan," Case said. "Let's go hunting angels. I got nothing better to do."

"Sounds good to me. Any leads?"

"Yeah, actually. I got a fix as soon as they dropped you off. Get some miles between you and that first fix, and I should be able to triangulate it down pretty tight."

"You're assuming the target is going to stay put. As I recall, Morningstar liked to move around."

"And you're assuming that the target is the Morningstar you knew—it's a whole 'nother universe, old buddy... we could both be wrong."

"True enough," I said. "How much of a baseline shift do you need?"

Case shrugged. "Could you manage maybe a hundred miles?"

"Sure."

* * * *

My primary mission was 'hunting angels.' My secondary mission was something that was either going to be a lot simpler... or basically impossible.

"I still think you got the wrong guy, Evangeia," I'd said. "I flunked out of history every time I took it."

"The requirements for a passing grade are fairly generous this time," Evangeia had replied. "It's an 'open book test.'"

My primary mission was now dependent upon getting some miles between me and where I had first appeared in this world. That was easily enough accomplished. In my own world, there was daily bus service between the Oregon coast and the Portland Metroplex. Here, it was a train, and it would be arriving in a place called 'Fort Vancouver.'

The miles were the same, though.

I promised Case I'd turn the social interface back on as soon as I got there. He was annoyingly needy about it, but I was firm. "You aren't even supposed to be in my head by proxy, dude. I definitely understand that it sucks to be you... but that's not exactly my problem, is it?"

"Not at all," Case replied. "Your problem is completing this mission without my help and dealing with the fact that your girlfriend only thought she'd lobotomized me."

"She's not my girlfriend, Case. Buh-bye."

It was a lot easier to think without Case projecting ghost images of himself into my implants. I actually did feel badly for him, for all that he'd done some pretty fucked-up shit to me. Whatever else might be said about getting shipped off to a parallel universe, I will say this: you get perspective.

I checked out of the hotel after grabbing breakfast in the lobby restaurant, paying with more 'fairy gold.' I was either going to need to get a part-time job soon or fabricate some more fake money. Credit card fraud also crossed my mind. They had 'credit cards' here, the systems supporting them were laughably simple. A real hacker from my Earth would've owned the whole damned planet—at which point, I would be obligated to take them into custody.

Sometimes it sucks being one of the good guys.

After breakfast, I confirmed that neither the train station nor the public library was where I expected them to be. Luckily, they were immediately nearby in locations next to each other that made a lot more sense than the 'Astoria' I'd once known. I stashed my belongings in a locker at the train station after purchasing a ticket for the trip inland. Then I nipped over to the library for a little research...
my 'secondary mission.'

All I really needed to do was read up on history with my implants set to record... and stay alive long enough to return and share the recording.

The people who care about such things wanted a simple answer to a not-so-simple question: they wanted to know when and how this world and my own had diverged. The fine theoretic points of this were lost on me... but I've always enjoyed hanging out in libraries.

I had already known that this version of Astoria was in a Pacific Northwest that had never been a part of the United States. It was remarkable to discover how little else had been. Should I wish to claim allegiance to anything approaching the place of my birth, I would be obliged to call myself a 'Texican' who had born in
'Greater Galveston.'

There was still a United States, but the differences outweighed the similarities. Everything looked about right in the kiddie history book I was reading, up to about 1830 or so. The maps looked about right as far west as the Mississippi. Past that, I didn't have a clue.

There were other differences as well in the history and current state of the world, but it was over my head. The History Channel ain't my thing.

Actually, here, it wasn't anybody's thing.

Evangeia had told me I would be effectively 'traveling in time.' I now knew what she meant.

The calendar pretty much reads the same. But in every other way, this was not the 21st century I knew and loathed. In some ways, it was more like the mid/late 20th... only not quite.

There were computers, there was an 'internet.' There were even cell phones. The whole damned thing tied together into a network of narcissists one-upping each other 140 bytes at a time? Not so much.

There were other differences as well. There were reasons why the gear I'd brought with me did not include a single shred of visible polycarbonate composite or advanced hydrocarbon-based plastic. Such things did not exist here.

Another thing that did not exist here was approximately half of my world's population. For a variety of reasons I didn't expect to understand any time soon, this version of Earth was holding steady at about three billion people, which had other tradeoffs as well. Global warming was a thing here as well—but it was not yet the unfolding disaster on the other side of the wormhole. Absent the Obligation I'd accepted, remaining in this world wouldn't be a bad thing.

Too bad I'd given my word.

I made a few mental notes for further research and decided to wrap up so I could grab some lunch before catching my train. Since it was convenient, I decided to grab a beer and a sandwich at the same hotel bar I'd hit the night before.

The same old guy was behind the bar. I didn't expect him to remember me, but he did.

"None of my business, son—but you planning on being in town for long?"

Son? The shit they'd given me was definitely doing the trick. "Actually, I'm on the afternoon train to Fort 'Coove. Why, what's up?"

"Had a couple of characters in here earlier asking a lot of questions. They wouldn't say who they were, but smelled like federales to me."

"What kind of questions?"

"Mostly just wanted to know about any strangers in town... then they got strange. Ever hear tell of a 'ghost airship'?"

four: kayce

As far as Pops was concerned, describing 'military intelligence' as a contradiction in terms was a joke that never got old—but as far as Pops is concerned, there are no old jokes; he'd still be telling 'knock-knocks' if he could get away with it.

But bad jokes aside, he's always been there for me, always supported my career. For all that, he was a typical Berkeley Communard who considered the California Navy an overpriced anachronism. "Kayce, darlin,' there's not gonna be more wars—not even the Estaditos are that crazy."

"Maybe so, maybe not," I'd replied. "You want to bet on the collective sanity of the U.S.? How about I throw in a deed for the Golden Gate Bridge as well?"

I admit it. I inherited Pop's sense of humor... if not his politics.

I'd mostly just joined the Navy to see the world anyway, agreed with Pops more than not on the likelihood of war. Where we mostly differed was on why there hadn't been a serious war in over a century. He seemed to think that humanity had somehow grown past it all... and I had known better than that long before the first time I ever sailed out of 'Frisco Bay.

After two overseas tours, I had taken a teaching position at the Academy and married my childhood sweetheart. Then came the offer from BSI— Bureau of Strategic Intelligence, sometimes also known as the 'Ferret Factory' or the 'Spook Works'... among other and less flattering things.

It was interesting work, and Pops would've hated it. The version of history I taught at the Academy only vaguely resembled the version under lock and key at the Bureau. The version he taught at Berkeley was, by comparison, not much more realistic than the 'scientific romances' he wrote in his spare time. It might've been disillusioning... if I'd had many illusions left after two active duty tours.

BSI fieldwork would've been worse, but no one was asking me to do that. The people referred to as 'spies' in bad fiction have qualifications I'm glad to lack. I suppose in some other world, I could've been the kind of person that gets dropped into a Central American jungle with a backpack full of gold, guns, and bad intentions. A good thing such worlds and people only exist in Pop's books. I wouldn't want to meet that person... much less be that person.

All in all, it was a pretty good life. Esmerelda loved the fact that I was connected enough to get us invited to the occasional society soirée and loved even better that my pay grade had finally gotten us past base housing. She resented my second office at BSI as much as my students were intrigued by it—but I could truthfully tell everyone that the work I did there wasn't that different from my published research... and not nearly as entertaining as anyone thought.

I was still considered 'active duty,' but short of the U.S. going completely crazy, the Brits or the Russians getting greedy again, or the Martians in Pop's books showing up, the most action I was ever likely to see wasn't going to go much past keeping my certifications up at the pistol range.

I should've known it would be the damned Martians.

five: murphy

I caught the train to Fort Vancouver without any complications from 'federales.' The overwhelming likelihood was that whoever had spooked my bartender wouldn't know a real 'ghost airship' from swamp gas. The likelihood of any of it having anything to do with me was even lower than the likelihood of me being here in the first place.

But it still left me with an uneasy sensation.

I picked up some more newspapers and a few magazines before I boarded the train, all of them on the trash/tabloid end of the literary spectrum. If a 'ghost airship' was what it sounded like, I needed to know about it. The mission I was on had been planned on the assumption that this version of Earth was relatively isolated from the multiverse at large, only recently available to alien intruders like me. If the other alien intruders I'd been sent to head off were already here, things might get complicated.

By the time I got off the train, I'd put enough miles behind me that Case should be able to get a triangulation fix on our target—which might or might not be a version of the stranded archangel who had once befriended me and called itself 'Lucifer Morningstar.' The heads-up display gear in my head still wasn't painting a target, though, which meant I was going to have to turn 'social' back on and talk to Case. I wasn't thrilled about dealing with the crazy cyborg son of a bitch, but at least I had the luxury of putting it off a little longer.

The stack of tabloids I'd read through on the train ride hadn't been as helpful as I'd hoped. I still couldn't say one way or the other if someone asking about ghost airships meant what I thought it might mean. As much as this version of Earth resembled a slightly backward version of mine, there were other ways in which it was oddly different. The major languages were all the same, but the vocabulary and idiom—at least in English—was just different enough, the history and assumptions just different enough... that I couldn't be sure.

There were just enough stories about things I would be inclined to call 'unidentified flying objects' to make me wonder—but also just enough weirdness in the detail to make me write it off as hysteria and urban folklore. Even in my version of Earth, where people like me had generated terabytes of disinformation to conceal the truth, there had been no shortage of people with overactive imaginations on hand to make my job easier. Could someone here be doing one of my old jobs for the same reasons I'd been doing it? Maybe.

An analog to The Order in this world wasn't really possible. For different reasons, an analog to 'The Company' was even less likely. This world's version of the United States had neither the reach nor the clout for any such thing—but that didn't rule out other actors with the same bad intentions. I just didn't know. But if this version of Earth was receiving visitors from Elsewhere, it had only just started—I was at least pretty sure of that much.

Add it to the list of research topics the next time I found myself in a library.

For reasons of my own, I decided to take local transportation south across the Columbia to the suburb known locally as 'New Boston.' I didn't really expect to see much of the city I'd retired to in another world... and I didn't. But there were odd outlines in common, for all the details differed. There was nothing remotely similar to the house I'd moved into to die, but the neighborhood was there—even if by a different name. I found a boarding house that I remembered from my own universe as a B&B. A few more coins of my fairy gold secured a room and a meal. A walk to a nearby park found a place where I could have a private conversation with a guy who wasn't really there.

I found a park bench on a hiking trail overlooking the Willamette. It was a cleaner river in this version of a place that was a coin toss away from being called 'Portland,' with fewer bridges and more water traffic.

I activated the 'social interface.' Case materialized on the other end of the bench I was sitting on. He still looked like an overaged club kid from the Nineties. "What, did you walk?" Case said. "You've been offline for days."

"You exaggerate—and not to put too fine a point on it, Case, you ain't the boss of me... and haven't been in a while. I'm running this operation."

I heard a dry chuckle in mind. "There is no 'operation' without me, old buddy."

"Call it a partnership, then—just remember that exactly one of us can walk away from this shit."

"Your girlfriend wouldn't like that."

"She ain't my girlfriend, Case—switching off in 5... 4... 3..."

"Okay! I apologize—partnership's fine!"

"Yeah, I kinda thought that might be the case."

"You know, you're still a punk rock cowboy asshole,"
Case sulked.

"No punks in this world," I replied.

Another dry chuckle in my mind. "There's at least one now. Want to know what I found?"

"Sure."

The heads-up display sprang into view. Case vanished, but I could still 'hear' him. "Your trip to 'Portland,' or whatever it's called, did the trick. I got a fix—furthermore, it's stable." Another blinking point appeared on the display. "Look familiar?" Case said.

"Yeah... actually."

"It should. You spent a lot of time in that part of the world—okay, not 'this' world, but our world's equivalent. Here, I believe it's called 'República Federal de Centroamérica.'"

I sighed. "Just tell me there's no cocaine trade and no revolutions."

The heads-up display winked out, and Case reappeared.
"I have no idea, old buddy. I just know that if you are serious about completing this mission... that's where you're going."

six: ellsberg

I hate it when I fall asleep wearing my glasses—but not as much as not being able to find them when I wake up. But it probably means I had a good night... that I'll eventually get around to remembering.

Last night must've been epic. I ransacked my apartment three times before I finally found them on the balcony under one of the deck chairs.

That bothered me. My glasses could've wound up in the street. It also bothered me that I didn't remember being out there. A replacement pair from Citizen Allotment would probably work better—I'm pretty sure my prescription needs updating—but it wouldn't be the same.
I like my old glasses: Citizen's Allotment doesn't do titanium frames or rose-colored gradient tint lenses.

Those old glasses remind me of better times.

I put the glasses on, finger combed my hair into place, and looked at myself in the bathroom mirror. I was still that sexy guy on the book jackets... well, almost.

Looking for coffee supplies in the kitchen, more of the evening began to fall into place. On the kitchen counter was an opened rejection letter on top of an unopened stack of bills, next to one empty and one half-empty bottle of Two Peso Chuck Rojo Formidable. There was also a matchbook from Harry's Cantina with a phone number scrawled on it.

I was wondering just how bad an idea it would be to call that number when someone started banging on my apartment door. It was too early to be the landlord; no one else had any business bothering me first thing in the morning. I ignored them, hoping they'd go away.

They didn't.

My head hurt too much for any such thing. "Uno momento," I yelled. "Por favor!" I snagged my bathrobe from the bedroom door, realized the sash was missing, decided I didn't care—if the shorts and singlet I'd slept in didn't suit whoever the hell was banging on my door, that was their problem.

I threw open the door. A small and very broad-shouldered young woman in Navy service blues was the source of the knocking. She had close-cropped blonde hair, a cleft chin, ice-blue eyes, and an expression that made her look like a pissed-off school teacher. Standing behind her were a pair of large and armed RCN Marines.

Whatever I didn't remember doing last night must have been epic, alright.

"Saul Ellsberg?" the woman asked.

"Well, yes."

"Sr. Ellsberg, I'm Commander Cullen, BSI. You are being taken into custody under Article Twelve, Section C of the California Espionage and Sedition Act. Anything you say from this point may be taken as evidence. You will be provided access to the abrogado of your choice. Formal charges are pending—but nonetheless, señor... you are coming with us."

Truly epic.

seven: murphy

The last time I'd been on this road, I was in an old car that had been supernaturally souped up to travel like a speeding bullet. No such luck this time around. I'd be lucky if I got thru this fucking desert at any speed above walking.

I'd traded the last of my 'fairy gold' for transportation and supplies, then made the necessary arrangements to make more. By the time I was anywhere where money mattered, I'd have as much as I needed. For now, the road south stretched ahead... not quite the same existential mirage as the last time I had ever seen it, but not far removed, either.

The motorcycle I straddled wasn't any brand I'd ever heard of, but the operating controls were similar enough to what I knew that I'd figured it out without any major road rash. The duster and rucksack I'd stepped into this world wearing were stashed in the sidecar. The goggles I'd found in the sidecar had an odd tint, but at least they kept crap out of my eyes. My old cycle jacket was earning its keep for the first time in decades.

I'd left the hiking staff back in Oregon and was now wearing another piece of the gear I'd brought from another universe: What looked like a local issue heavy service revolver, with some additional features that might or might not come in handy, now holstered to my leg. 'Strapped and loaded' was neither a political statement here nor a compensation mechanism for over-aged adolescents. But in the empty high desert between Oregon and Texas, it wasn't exactly a bad idea, either.

* * * *

Finding a decent ride had taken a few days.

I've always been good at figuring out how to blend in or at least be an anomaly that made sense. Back in the day, working black ops for The Company, I'd never tried to pass myself off as a local. I was always just another half-gringo who'd had some bad luck in El Norte and had to leave. Later, I'd found similarly plausible ways to pass myself off as 'just some IT guy' after I'd taken a desk job.

There was no way I was going to fit smoothly into this version of 'Cascadia,' but I'd figured out what ought to be a plausible dodge... at least as long as I didn't run into any real 'Texicans.'

After Case had told me where I was going, I decided it was time for some more research. The mere fact that I had spent more time on the ground in another version of the place than I ever wanted to think about... that meant nothing. I needed to know what it would take to get around discreetly in this world's version of the same thing.

Of course, there was no Powell's Books in 'New Boston,' but there was a decent public library system. The closest branch to my boarding house had a nice travel section, plenty of history books, and even a section labeled 'Esoterica'—which looked like a good place to read up on ghost airships, were I so inclined. There were also local newspapers and 'Net Terminals'—no mouse, different keyboard, ugly screen. But I could figure them out.

It didn't take me long to find what I needed. The best deal I could find on a used bike was in what I would've called 'Southwest Portland' in another world, even further out in the suburbs. After a brief online exchange with the seller, l had an appointment to check out the goods.

I spent the rest of the afternoon reading up on this world's versions of the American Southwest and Central America. As long as I was careful, I didn't see any problems getting around. The kind of stupid shit I would've run into crossing the Rio Grande in my universe wasn't going to happen here. Things could get complicated if I ever had to visit 'The United States of America,' but nothing on my itinerary involved going that far east... at least not for now.

I went ahead and closed out at my boarding house, then took a water taxi and a streetcar to go check out the bike. I'd either find other cheap accommodations or kip out in a park someplace. I hadn't slept rough in a long time, but I suspected I'd be doing a lot of it fairly soon. I decided to get used to the idea.

The bike seller's directions involved taking the streetcar all the way to the end of the line and then walking a mile or so to the seller's shop. By the time I got off the streetcar,
I was pretty much back in the woods. The end of the line trolley stop was across the street from a railway terminal,

the two of them surrounded by a cluster of stores and a few bars.

A sign over the terminal building read 'Multnomah'—which, I suppose, was more or less where I was. A bridge spanned a crystal clear creek, a handful of streets disappeared into the woods. I was largely returned to the Northwest rainforest. Had a sasquatch greeted me, I wouldn't have been much surprised... for all that they weren't supposed to be in this universe.

The invention of combustion engines and discovery of oil as an energy source hadn't differed in broad outline in this world's history, even though different guys' names were on the patents. There was a wide range of two, three, four, and even six wheeled personal transports on this world's roads—more similar than not to what I was used to. Millions of people driving millions of cars they couldn't afford and couldn't live without... that hadn't happened, although the United States was still pretty lousy with them.

From what I'd read, the United States was pretty lousy in general.

I was still figuring it all out, but what I would've called 'the Civil War' had happened a generation earlier and turned out different—a lot worse for the South, with hangings, reparations, and decades of military occupation. Texas had stayed a republic, California became one as well, everything else west of the Mississippi wound up as border states and territories that got traded like poker chips for most of the 19th century. California wound up federated with Hawai'i and was even more 'liberal' than the one in my world. Except for the fact it went all the way to the Canadian border, 'Texas' sounded a lot like the one I was from, with the exception of little details like having its own air force.

In some ways, getting from Oregon to Central America was going to be easier here than in my world, in some ways harder—but I was definitely going to need some decent transportation that wasn't too picky about the definition of 'road.'

The road I was taking to get that transportation redefined itself as I got deeper into the woods. The paving ended before the road did, but the gravel that took its place was hardpacked and well-used.

The 'mechanic shop' looked like it had started out as a barn—not too surprising, since it was sitting in front of what looked like a farm. Vehicles and farm implements in varying states of repair surrounded the garage-like front door, which was open.

Since it was open, I walked in. "Hola," I said to no one in particular.

A kid in coveralls emerged from the back, wiping his hands with a shop rag. "Hi," he said. "Can I help you?"

"Here to see a man about a bike... Carl around?"

"I'm Carl," the kid said. "You're Murphy, right?"

I took a second look. At first glance, I'd thought I was looking at a tall twelve-year-old. I could see now he was older, maybe fifteen or sixteen. Maybe a little young to be selling bikes, but I hadn't been too young to steal a couple at a comparable age. This kid, though, was nothing like the rough little customer my daddy had taken pains to set straight. He was almost girlishly slender, with a mop of ash blond hair and an utterly deadpan expression. "Yeah, I'm Murphy," I told him.

The kid nodded. "Bike's back here."

There was even more junk in the back of the shop, most of which looked like it was in the process of either getting fixed or dismantled. I saw something that caught my attention. "Hey, what about this?"

"That's not the bike we're talking about," Carl said. "I just got that one at an auction... needs fixing."

What I'd noticed was another motorcycle, bigger than the one I'd seen online, with a sidecar and an oddly mottled gray paint job.

"How much 'fixing'?"

"I was planning on getting the parts with what you're paying me for the Road Chief."

"Do you ever make any money, kid?"

Carl shrugged. "I do alright. What do you want the bike for?"

"Road trip, crosscountry."

"It's a better bike, but I can't fix it until I sell the other one."

"How does this sound? I buy this one, buy the parts, and pay you to fix it."

"That's almost as much as a new bike."

"Would it be as good?"

He shook his head. "No."

"I didn't think so. Make me an offer."

eight: kayce

"Okay, people—that paper on the second Burr Administration is still due on Tuesday. I expect it to be long on strategy and very short on dueling practices. 'Net message me if you have any questions. Class dismissed."

I was stuffing papers into my briefbag and thinking about a latte between classes when my phone started buzzing. When I saw who it was, I realized the latte was going to have to wait.

The Academy and the Bureau are both in the old part of the East Bay Naval Preserve. It's a short walk... even though it might as well be a walk between different worlds.

My jefe at the Bureau was the old man himself, Hiram Díaz. Most of the research I did for him didn't really need to be classified but wound up that way anyhow. Californianos aren't like Estaditos. We never really wanted to have a Navy in the first place, don't particularly want to run the world, would rather not know what it takes to make sure no one else is trying to run it either. So, the Bureau keeps a lot of things quiet... and keeps an eye on people who might otherwise be a problem.

I don't often get called into Admiral Díaz's office at the BSI building. When I do, it's usually for a good reason. Usually means having to tell Esmerelda to have dinner without me. I was hoping this was not going to be one of those occasions, but you never know. They call it the 'Ferret Factory' for a good reason.

I had to badge in twice to get to the office—once in the building lobby, once when I got off the elevator. The smiling middle-aged woman who waved me into the admiral's office may have looked less intimidating than the armed Marine I had to get past in the lobby, but—given the choice—I would take on the Marine in a heartbeat. Like myself, Mathilde taught part-time at the Academy—unarmed combat, in her case. Her black belts had black belts.

Admiral Hiram Díaz is a great brick of a man with wavy gray hair, olive skin, and deep distaste for the Standard Uniform Code. On this occasion, he was wearing deck shoes, dungarees, and a watch sweater. It could've just as easily have been a flight suit, or anything else RCN issue that didn't require a tie or a starched collar. Glasses with antique gold wire rims were perched atop the wavy gray hair.

As usual, his office was strewn with papers, all marked as 'top secret' or above, that Mathilde would eventually refile in the collection of reinforced steel cabinets in the back of the office. "Hola, Kayce," he said, offhandedly returning my salute. "I appreciate you coming over so quickly. Care for some coffee?"

"No thanks, sir." The admiral had family from Louisiana and had acquired from them a taste for something called 'chicory.' I hadn't thought you could make Navy break room coffee taste worse. I had been wrong.

"As you like. Have a seat." Helping himself to some of the vile stuff, the admiral returned to his desk—sweeping a pile of reconnaissance photos to the floor in the process. "I'll try not to keep you long. I know you have another afternoon class."

"No worries, Admiral. I gave it to my teaching assistant."

"Ah, better yet." Sipping his coffee, the admiral glanced around his office for a moment, then pulled a file jacket from a pile of them in a spare chair. "So, I do have an assignment for you. It's a little complicated, though."

"They usually are, sir."

"This one perhaps more than usual. There's a story I'd like to share that might help put it in context."

Good thing I'd handed off my afternoon class.

"This goes back several decades," he continued. "Back when there was a project to develop a fission bomb. Do you ever read any Sci-Rom?"

"Not often, sir—it's usually a little long on the 'rom' and short on the 'sci,' for my taste."

Díaz nodded. "Not always, though... and that's rather the point of this story. Toward the end of the fission bomb project, a piece turned up in one of the bigger Sci-Rom magazines. It was all about some imaginary planet where a couple of countries were at war and in a race to develop a new weapon... that just happened to be a fission bomb."

"That's not too surprising," I said. "The theory was fairly well known."

"Well, what was surprising was the level of technical detail in the story. It pretty much outlined every piece of engineering our project had found necessary to build a fission bomb. My predecessor in this office was alarmed—enough to send agents to interview both the magazine publisher and the author. She was convinced there must have been a security leak."

"And was there?"

"No, not at all. It turned out that the writer was simply very well-read and had a good imagination. We still had to suppress it, of course. By that time, the Admiralty had decided that a 'fission bomb' was simply too dangerous to build. The F-bomb project was canceled, and rightly so. If we'd built one, the Yanquis probably would've taken a shot at it as well, and so would the Russkies. In no time at all, we would've had the U.S. and Russia dropping F-bombs all over the place... can't have that."

"No, sir." There was no hurrying the great man. He would reach a point with this when he felt like it. The prospect of dinner with my wife was beginning to seem remote.

"And that brings us to this." He unclasped the file jacket, extracted a garishly colored magazine, and passed it over the desk to me. I recognized it: it was one of Pop's favorites. The cover featured a painting of an arid desert. In the sky above the desert, a disk-shaped object was hurtling downward and spouting flames.

"A gentleman named Saul Ellsberg was responsible for the cover story, 'Encounter at Corona.' Interesting story: It's all about a supposed spaceship crash in the scrubby backend of Texas, with the spaceship and the remains of the crew passing from Texas and into the hands of the U.S. government—which then sets up a top-secret project to figure out how the spaceship works.

"The story was apparently a big hit with the magazine's readers—so much so that Sr. Ellsberg wrote a sequel." The admiral reached into the folder again and pulled out a typed manuscript. "It gets even better in the sequel, which ties the crash to the great 'Ghost Airship' hoax of the 1890s and sets the whole thing up as the prelude to an alien invasion. That's where we come in."

Finally. Maybe I wouldn't be eating cold leftovers after all. "I'm not sure I understand, sir."

"Your immediate assignment is to bring in this Sr. Ellsberg and find out where he's getting his information. Effective immediately, you are promoted to Commander and receiving gold-alpha level security clearance."

"Admiral, I could swear you just told me I'm being promoted so I can interrogate a sci-rom writer about an imaginary invasion by imaginary aliens."

"The only thing you heard wrong was the 'imaginary' part, Kayce. It's all true. All of it. Welcome to the single biggest secret you will ever know."

nine: murphy

"So, let me just make sure I've got this right. You're paying my son to restore a used motorcycle you just bought from him, you want to rent a room from me while he's doing it, and you're paying for all of this out of pocket with California Gold Pesos. Anything I overlooked?"

"Just the part about I just ordered another beer," I replied. "Seadog's good."

"Sure. Why not?" The woman behind the bar was of middle years, younger than my real age, dark-haired, and full-figured. She had the same green eyes as her son.

"Magdalena Ivanov," she had said when I first arrived, offering me her hand. "Folks around here call me Maggie." Maggie was wearing black jeans, a low-cut black tank top, and a dark blue flannel shirt that paired well with silver and turquoise jewelry.

Despite Carl's best efforts at undercutting himself, I had finally reached an acceptable deal with him on the other bike. I honestly think the kid would've paid me if he'd had to—he just liked fixing things. I'd known people like him before. I kept thinking he reminded me of someone, but I was damned if I could figure out who it was.

I gave him a healthy advance and asked him if he knew of any place in the neighborhood I could stay for a few days. The boarding houses all over the north end of Fort Vancouver were a little harder to find out here in the sticks. But I caught a lucky break.

"My mom's got a room over in the village," Carl told me. "It's over a bar, though."

I assured him I had no problem whatever with crashing over a bar. He called his mom and then gave me directions that pretty much led me straight back to the trolley stop.

'Maggie's Place' was low-keyed and unpretentious, a typical Pacific Northwest neighborhood pub in any universe, sandwiched between a general store and a post office. Happy hour had just kicked in when I showed up.

Maggie drew a pint and handed it to me. "Gold's good, Sr. Murphy, and we're happy to have it. Just don't think it answers all questions... or that any amount of it will help you if you deal poorly with my son."

"Oh, I wouldn't think that for a minute," I told her, taking the beer. "Carl thinks he can get that bike fixed up in a week or so. I figure it might be quicker than that if I help him. Then I'll be on my way. By the way, 'Señor Murphy' was my daddy—I'm just Murphy."

"Fair enough, 'Just Murphy,'" she said. "Mind if I ask where you're headed?"

"Texas, for starters. I was born there, haven't been back in a while. Past that, I'm still figuring it out."

"You don't sound much like a Texican."

"Well, like I said... it's been a while."

* * * *

Eventually, I made my way up to the room I'd rented. Maggie's regulars had all been curious about the new guy sitting at the bar, but no one asked any questions I hadn't been able to answer with either an evasion or an offer to buy the next round.

The next day, I would be making my way back out to Carl's shop and seeing what I could do to help him get the bike I'd bought road worthy. It was definitely a better deal than the one I'd first bid on. It was military surplus, originally built by an outfit called 'Armstrong Canadien' for the Republic of California Corps of Marines. This meant nothing to me, but Carl thought highly of it. It also explained the paint job, which was apparently this world's version of camouflage. All of the parts could be sourced locally.

There was something I really needed to do before packing it in for the evening that hardly required me to be sober at all. Pouring a drink from the bottle I'd bought when I closed out my tab, I activated the 'social' interface on my implants. Once again, the ghost image of Colvin Case materialized on a random piece of furniture. "We need to talk," I said.

"Sure thing, old buddy." Case's avatar was still firmly stuck in the 90s, but he'd switched it up a bit, trading out the Hawai'ian shirt for a denim hoodie and a black t-shirt.

"Target is holding firm, hasn't moved."

"That's not what I'm talking about. There are a couple of things I need to know."

114

"At least a couple, but I'll do what I can."

"First, just how private is this circuit? I was told two-way real-time communication through the wormhole wasn't even possible."

"It's not," Case replied. "This is all in your head—just not in the way you might think."

I poured another drink. "Okay, I'm listening."

"You probably have no idea how much raw storage capacity you've been walking around with since you got upgraded from the farm team. It's a lot. Enough that I could upload myself a few terabytes at a time while you were in cold storage, and no one was paying attention. The only thing that's coming through in real-time is the targeting data—just like they said."

"So... I'm essentially talking to a computer virus in my fucking head. Funny, I don't remember opening any suspicious emails."

Case chuckled. "I'm more than just a virus, old buddy. You might want to remember back in the day when we both worked for The Company. You were pretty good with computers... but not like I was."

He wasn't exaggerating. Case would've been one dead fucking club kid if anyone had ever sent him on an operation, but he'd been a bona fide hacker long before a generation of pimply misfits and assorted criminals gave the word a bad name. He'd given it up when they moved him into management, but he definitely had skills—that may or may not have had something to do with the whole 'space alien hybrid' thing. "Okay," I said. "I'll buy it. Why?"

Case looked at my drink. "Wish I could have one of those—or anything, for that matter. You really have no idea what your girlfr—excuse me, what

The Order has been doing to me for nearly twenty years. It has not been fun."

"Neither was what you did to me, which is the other thing I wanted to ask you about."

Case sighed. "I figured that was going to come up at some point."

"Goddam right. You made me hallucinate a replay of every... fucking... day of the year it took my marriage to fall apart, minus the few happy bits. Not just once—again and again and again, until I finally broke out of it the only way I could. I don't know how much of that was planned, how much of it was suggestion, how much of it was some shit you improvised on the spot. But if you plan on being a welcome guest in my head, you got some explainin' to do."

"Yeah, I suppose I do." The avatar got up and walked around the room. The illusion was as perfect as the ones he'd once tortured me with. He wound up at the window, looking out. I had to wonder what, if anything, he really 'saw.'

"I know you didn't just sell drugs back in the day. You ever do anything really shitty when you were high?" he finally asked me.

"Nope—and please don't tell me you were strung out on coke while you were mindfucking me."

He laughed. "No, I was strung out on 'mindfucking' you. The best coke or smack in the world pales by comparison... not that you'd know anything about it. And I was being controlled as well. You want me to say I'm sorry? Fine, 'I'm sorry.' But the last time I checked, you got over it. And I've been a goddamned lab specimen ever since that shit happened. Once I figured out I could hack your implant, I downloaded myself so I could escape... except, of course, I really didn't."

"What do you mean?" I asked him.

"I mean that the 'real me' is still back in that lab in Greenland being mutated into a better part for a cyborg weapon system for the little war you signed up for, old buddy—the same war 'the Fortuned' or whatever else they call themselves plan on bringing here.

"You think you got some issues over the shit I did to you? I have some serious issues with the 'people,' the high and mighty damned space elves, that have done far worse to me daily since the last time you ever saw me as a man."

"Then why are you helping them? And why are either one of us here?"

The ghost of my old friend laughed. "You're here because you got sold a bill of goods. I'm here because it's the only game in town, and it beats where I was all to shit. We'll complete your mission, old buddy—I got no problem with that. Just do us both one serious favor. Think long and hard before you activate any of the gadgets in that bag. Better yet, just make delivery and get out... fast."

ten: ellsberg

They were nice about it. No handcuffs; I even got to get dressed. But any thought that I was going anywhere besides where that butch little Navy officer and her portable wall of Marines wanted me to go... was too foolish to bother thinking.

There was barely enough room in the lift for all four of us. The marines reeked of disdain and regulation aftershave despite carefully blank expressions behind regulation Navy sunglasses. I found myself realizing, very inappropriately, that the butch little officer had a nice backside that

Navy tailoring did nothing to hide. Lucky it was a short ride to the ground floor. Luckier yet that they'd let me get dressed.

Sitting in the street in front of my building was an unmarked RCN staff car. The officer with the cute caboose sat in front with the driver, and I found myself squeezed into the back between the Marines. Why I was being arrested was beyond me, much less by military police. Unless passing the occasional bad check at a bar had become an act of treason, this had to be some sort of mistake.

More of the night before was coming back to me; it was nothing out of the ordinary. I'd hit Harry's and a couple of other places. Eventually, the sense of disappointment went away, and I realized I could go home, polish off some more wine, and be able to sleep through the night... which was sort of the whole idea in the first place. There's other ways to get a decent night's sleep, but I know what works for me.

I won't say that I sat back and enjoyed the ride. I distracted myself by watching the scenery. Not surprisingly, we were crossing to the East Bay and the Naval Preserve. I'd driven cabs a few times and got to know the route pretty well. I usually worked late shifts. Sailors on shore leave who couldn't wait for a train were always good for a tip, sometimes a drink as well.

Once we were on the base itself, I lost any sense of direction. But I did recognize the RCN admin tower when we arrived. Next to it was an older and smaller building; next to both, a parking garage. The staff car parked in the garage, and I was led to the older building. The Marines escorted me as far as a security gate in the lobby, then fell back as Commander Cullen badged me through and into a lift. This one was big enough that I didn't have to stand directly behind Commander Cullen's nicely curved posterior... but I still found myself thinking about it.

We exited the lift into an office foyer manned by a pleasantly plump woman who looked like she was probably my age. She waved us through another security gate and into a small conference room. "Please sit," Commander Cullen said. "May I offer you a beverage?"

What I really wanted was that half bottle of Two Peso Chuck back at my apartment, but I would take what I could get. "Coffee would be great," I said.

"Do you like chicory?"

"Never heard of it."

"In that case, I hope you like cream and sugar."

eleven: murphy

It still took over a week to get the bike up to speed.

Although I'd been serious about helping Carl with the work, I mainly just wanted to watch as much of what he did as possible. Historical research wasn't the only thing my implants could be set to record. I wanted to make sure I could do field maintenance on something my life was going to wind up depending on.

Carl had wanted to paint the bike as well, but except for touching up some rust spots, I talked him out of it. I was going to be going into places where a low profile was highly advisable. The less my ride looked worth stealing, the better.

It reminded me of older, better days of when my daddy had tried his best to interest me in the finer points of being a mechanic—except that this time, it was the old guy that was the learner. He would've had better luck with Carl. The kid was apparently self-taught and had as much of an aptitude for machinery as I'd had for getting into trouble.

The farm behind the shop was owned and worked by Maggie's parents, who reminded me more than a little of my own folks. Maybe there's a universe out there where I was the lonely savant kid fixing bikes on my grandpa's farm instead of a little thug who turned into a big thug who just happened to also be good with various forms of digital and not-so-digital sorcery. It's a big multiverse... everything is possible.

When I wasn't working on the bike, I was mostly hanging out at Maggie's Place or a couple of other joints in what everyone in the vicinity just called 'the village.' I'd decided I was done with alternate history research for a while. I'd either report back with what I had or not.

The 'cosmetic changes' I'd been promised when I got juiced on the moon were continuing to kick in. I decided to change my look. If I was going to be riding across the desert on the closest thing this world had to a Harley, I was going to look the part. I shaved the beard but left the sideburns. Since I apparently wasn't bald anymore, I'd already stopped shaving my head. The hair that was growing back wasn't the color I'd had as a kid, but it wasn't gray either. And it was growing back a lot faster than I'd expected.

The folks at Maggie's Place were hardly any different from anyone else I had drank with across three decades and two universes in the Pacific Northwest. There might've been more lumberjacks and fewer web developers, but the wardrobe choices were about the same. The beer was just as good... and a damned sight less pretentious. 'Californianos' were as little loved here as they had been back at the Lyin' Lamb, for pretty much the same reasons; the world west of the Cascades was considered a foreign country with even better reason.

As a half-Irish/half-Mexican guy from Texas, I was an entertaining novelty. As a stranger passing through town who didn't mind standing the occasional round, I was treated as a friend.

I got the backstory on Maggie Ivanov one of the evenings I chose to drink at the somewhat seedier competing tavern across the street.

"Everyone called him 'Crazy Ivan,'" the bartender told me.

"Why's that?" I asked.

"Some people just don't know what they want, don't mind messing up other folks lives while they figure it out. Also, he walked out on Maggie—if that isn't crazy, I don't know what the fuck is. You about ready for another?"

"Sure." The bartender, a burly, long-haired guy who looked about my apparent age, drew me a pint and kept talking.

"We eventually sort of figured it out... after a couple of Californiano feds with an extradition warrant showed up lookin' for him. That's when Maggie found out about the other 'Señora Ivanov' down in East Bay 'Frisco. She was not pleased."

"I expect not," I said, taking the pint.

Vladimir Ivanov sounded like an interesting guy who I probably would've taken great pleasure in throwing out of a bar if I was still in that line of work. A machinist's mate in the Russian merchant marine, Ivanov might've even been serious about settling down in the Willamette Valley and running a repair shop and a bar—to the extent he was serious about much of anything.

It just hadn't turned out that way.

It wasn't any of my business, and I wasn't planning on being around long enough for it to matter one way or the other. But I wanted to make sure I didn't accidentally say the wrong thing or piss anyone off.

I had already come close to it.

* * * *

The previous night, I had been sitting in Maggie's place when a random question came to mind. "You run this place by yourself, right?" I had asked.

"I'm not the only bartender," Maggie had replied. "You've been here enough nights to know that."

"That's not exactly what I mean," I replied. Maggie was sitting behind the bar with her feet on a barstool, leaning back against the wall. I was on the other side of the bar, leaning on the same wall. Except for a couple of kids playing video poker, we pretty much had the place to ourselves. "Carol and Dave are nice folks. Not everyone who shows up on the other side of the bar is 'nice folks.'"

"Actually, everyone who shows up at this bar is either nice folks or they find someplace else to drink. This is just a neighborhood tavern, Murphy. If you're looking for something more exciting, there's places down by the river that might be a little more to your liking. If you're looking for a job, I appreciate the thought—but I don't need a bouncer... or a man telling me how to run my business."

"Apologies, Señora. No offense intended."

"None taken, and sorry if I'm a little touchy. And I'm not a 'Señora'—this ain't California, regardless what the Californianos might think. I'm either 'Maggie' or 'Mrs. Ivanov.'"

I'd already pissed her off, but I had to ask, anyway. "I'm surprised you kept his name."

"It's Carl's name, too, until he decides otherwise. Maybe I just keep it to remind myself not to repeat the same mistake."

"Again, no offense."

She smiled. "And again, none taken. And—also, no offense—but you remind me of him."

"I'm not offended, but I am finding it unlikely… 'Mrs. Ivanov.'"

"I'm not talking about your looks, 'Señor Murphy.' You're a charming man who is more than a little vague on where he's from, even vaguer on where he's going, somehow has enough money to get there, and doesn't even have a vague explanation of where the money comes from. So, yeah… I'm a little reminded of someone."

I chuckled. "At least I manage to be 'charming' as well."

"Oh, you are… but that's pretty much where the resemblance ends. At the end of the day, it was pretty easy to figure Vlad out. I don't think that would be true of you, even if you weren't 'just passing through.'"

"I'm not that complicated."

"Maybe, maybe not—but you don't make any sense, Murphy. When you got here, I thought you were my age or older. Now, I'd say my age or younger."

"Shaving a beard will do that."

"I suspect there's more to it than that. Just don't wind up Carl's age—I suspect you'd be a bad influence."

I laughed, but it was an uneasy laugh. I didn't expect I'd rejuvenate down to the juvenile delinquent level… but who knew?

* * * *

"What kind of tattoo is that?"

We were in front of the shop, making final adjustments to the bike's drivetrain. It was a warm day, and I'd shed my outer shirt. The Mark of Obligation I'd received in barter for my second life was visible below the short sleeves of my undershirt. Carl was still wearing the coveralls I had never seen him without. Tattoos were not as commonplace in this version of the Pacific Northwest, but neither were they rare.

"Let's just say it has cultural significance," I replied. "And it means that I'm part of something."

"What, like a gang?" Carl said.

I laughed. "Do I look like a gangster?"

"I dunno, maybe."

"If you think that, why are you helping me?"

"You're paying me. Also, I asked Mom. Mom said it was okay."

"Really? What else did she say?"

"She said you're a lost soul looking to get found and that helping you was good karma." Carl handed me a wrench and stared into the toolbox for a long moment. "She also said she likes you."

"Your mom's good folks, Carl. So are you."

"Are you really going to Texas?"

"Among other places, yeah."

"I'd like to take a trip like that one of these days." A far-away look crossed his eyes, and I suddenly realized who he reminded me of. I found myself imagining him with
an overloaded backpack and an urgent desire to see the world.

I swallowed hard, considering yet again the utter improbability of my own life, the growing list of people who had been a part of it and never would be again. "One of these days, you will. You need to get a little older and a little bigger. Actually... a lot bigger."

* * * *

I had planned on slipping out discreetly. The bike was parked in the alley behind Maggie's Place. I had settled up with Maggie and Carl. I'd invested what remained of my fairy gold in supplies for my journey and started a new batch.

I didn't get to slip out discreetly.

The people I'd been drinking with for the last week and some change apparently had decided they liked me well enough to see me off. The send-off was at Maggie's, where I was informed my money was no good— a good thing, given that the next batch was still cooking.

Even the regulars from the other bars in the village showed up. It got rowdy. It got fun. Maggie had pulled a bottle of extremely old and wicked single malt scotch from below the bar, from which we all did thimble-sized shots every time a keg blew. A local band was set up in the corner—a trio: mandolin, fiddle, upright bass.

Not surprisingly, there was a pretty decent line for the toilet well before midnight. Not one to stand on ceremony, I felt free to take advantage of the alley.

Toward the end of the evening, I found myself in the alley and found I had company. Josh, the bartender from across the street, apparently had the same need and the same idea.

"I did you a favor, man," he said.

"You did," I replied. "Thank you for not pissing on my bike."

"No problem, but that ain't what I mean."

"Okay... tell me about it."

"I told the feds you were headed north."

"Uhh... what feds?"

"The feds that were in my bar last night," he replied. "They wanted to know two things."

"Let me guess," I said. "The other thing was 'ghost airships,' right?"

"Yup—what the fuck is that shit?"

"It's complicated."

twelve: kayce

The first airships had been cumbersome and slow-moving, barely more than gasbags pushed through the air by fans. Decades would pass before ships of the air could compete in any meaningful way with ships of the sea or with railroads.

Unless they were ghost airships.

The Great Airship Hoax of 1890 was considered a textbook example of new technology creating myths and folklore. Bored telegraph operators amused themselves by creating stories of mysterious airships that could fly at great speeds, hover, and even become invisible. Newspapers picked up the stories, and in a matter of weeks, there was scarcely anywhere in greater North America where people did not report 'ghost airship' sightings... perhaps not surprisingly, nowhere more than Texas.

Except it wasn't a hoax.

"The Bureau didn't exist then, but we inherited the archives of our predecessors," Admiral Díaz told me. "Reports from that period involving trained observers are fairly striking. The stories that wound up in the papers were fantastic... but clearly, there was real phenomena behind it all."

"I'm surprised there has never been a serious investigation," I replied. I still couldn't say 'ghost airship' with a straight face, but I was taking my cues from the admiral—whose face was absolutely stone serious. We were sitting in Díaz's office. On a televisor that hadn't been there before, we could see the sci-rom writer I'd brought in for questioning, in the room where we would shortly be joining him. The usual clutter of unfiled state secrets on Díaz's desk had been pushed to one side to make room for Ellsberg's manuscript, a couple of file jackets, and the magazine with Ellsberg's story.

"No real need," the admiral said. "And the Navy had a few other priorities back then."

"Any theories as to what these things really were?"

"Lots of them, ranging from secret aircraft built by the Russian Empire to being the work of some deranged genius inventor in the U.S."

"Or having somehow gotten here from Mars," I said.

Admiral Díaz might have been serious about this, but he was not happy. "Correct, Commander... or that."

Pops would love this. Too bad I couldn't tell him a word of it.

By the time 'ghost airships' returned in the nineteen forties, a few things had changed.

The Treaty of Vera Cruz had settled who was the dominant power in North America, aviation had evolved significantly, and the Services Consolidation Act of 1920 put the Navy squarely in charge of military aeronautic development in California. The Act also created the Bureau of Strategic Intelligence.

And there was also a new name for the 'phenomena.'

"A full ninety percent of the 'mystery disk' reports from the 1940s were either natural phenomena or misidentified RCN test aircraft," Admiral Díaz said. "The remaining ten percent were... problematic."

Thanks to Pop's regrettable weakness for the pulps, Ghost Airships and Mystery Disks were not new concepts to me. But the idea of BSI taking such things seriously was going to take some getting used to.

Among other things.

"The 'Multilateral American Joint Exotic Science and Technology Investigation Commission'? No offense, Admiral—but who comes up with these things?"

Díaz shrugged. "It's a joint operation, and the Yanquis have an excessive fondness for acronyms. I wouldn't worry too much about it, commander.

You're under standing orders to deny that M.A.J.E.S.T.I.C. even exists... much less admit being assigned to it."

"Works for me, sir." Indeed, it did. Among other things, it would spare me having to explain to my wife that I would be working with those people. My Esmerelda is a kind and tolerant woman. But like the admiral, her ancestry was almost exclusively 'original' Californiano. Unlike Díaz, she did not use the 'Y word' in casual conversation, considered it just as vulgar as 'gringo.' On the other hand, she and I would not even be considered 'married' by the vast majority of Estaditos. Tolerance works best when it's a two-way street.

The commission had been formed in the aftermath of the Corona Incident... another hoax that wasn't.

In 1947, a seven-day wonder story had involved the supposed crash of a 'mystery disk' in a remote part of Texas. The Texas Air Corps went so far as to send a press release to local papers, followed days later by a retraction. To the world at large, it was just one more bit of craziness out of a corner of North America not exactly known for a tight grip on reality.

To the smaller world I was now part of, the story was even crazier—not least of which for being true.

"The cover story was that the Tejanos had misidentified a crashed RCN advanced prototype as... something else," Admiral Díaz said. "The reality is that they had it right the first time."

I picked up the copy of Thrilling Science Stories featuring Ellsberg's cover story. "So this is not fiction?"

"Fairly bad fiction, actually... but many of the details track almost exactly to events as we know them." The admiral picked up the manuscript. "This one is marginally better, but we do not collect these things for their literary quality. Ever since the F-bomb project was coincidentally exposed by a Sci-Rom magazine, the Bureau has made a point of keeping an eye on these publications for possibly useful intelligence. Sr. Ellsberg's first story put him on the watch list. When the sequel turned up, I requested its rejection and had it sent in."

"I had no idea the Bureau was so chummy with the Sci-Rom community, sir."

"No need to know, Commander—at least before your present assignment. We even occasionally plant stories in these publications when there is a need. I am reasonably certain the Brits, Russkies, and Yanquis do the same thing."

"In that case," I said, "are we sure this man Ellsberg is not on someone's payroll?"

The admiral picked up one of the file jackets, which had Ellsberg's name on the spine. "If so, he is the most well-concealed operative who has ever lived. He is fully documented as having spent his entire life right here in San Francisco. It is not a remarkable or exceptional life. Prior to his literary career, he seems to have held many occupations without having ever achieved recognition or success in any of them. His work as a writer seems to be following that pattern as well."

I looked up at the televisor. For a man who had been hauled out of bed at gunpoint with an apparent massive hangover, Saul Ellsberg was remarkably composed. Under my Marines' supervision, he'd dressed, choosing a tweed suit and broadcloth shirt that suited his supposed profession. He had thinning hair in a style that had once been fashionable, a face and expression that reminded me of a basset hound, including the sad brown eyes. He very much looked like a middle-aged hack writer who'd seen better days.

But even so, he had dignity.

"And the second story?" I asked, picking up the manuscript. The title on the cover page read 'Armada of Ghosts.'

"The second story is why he's here," the admiral said. "Even more details about things the Majestic group has kept secret for decades—made worse by bad timing."

"Timing, sir?"

"Timing, Commander. Sr. Ellsberg's could not have been worse. The world has become strange, strange has perhaps become normal. These things—ghost airships, mystery disks—whatever you want to call them, are part of a larger and disturbing pattern. You are one of the best analysts I have—do you not see it?"

"A lot of what I see in the world at large these days doesn't seem to make a lot of sense, sir," I replied. "But if there is a larger pattern to it, I may not be the analyst you think I am."

"And I am perhaps too much immersed in what I admit to be a unique perspective," the admiral said. "And that is one of the reasons you are here. But if what believe I see is true, we may well be in the early stages of what I can only describe as... an invasion."

thirteen: ellsberg

The coffee helped. A gallon or so of it would've helped even more.

The tough little RCN officer had left me in a conference room without so much as a word about when I would get to call my abrogado... or anything else.

On the one hand, I was a citizen of the Republic of California. I had committed no crimes, had nothing—well, nothing much to hide. On the other hand, I had just been arrested anyway by the Navy's Bureau of Strategic Intelligence—the professional paranoids who considered the safekeeping of the Republic their personal responsibility. Innocence was not going to help me if they considered me some sort of threat.

It had been almost an hour. I wanted more coffee. I also wanted to piss. Either the door was locked, or it wasn't. There was either a guard outside the door... or there wasn't. I could at least knock on the damned door and give it a try... right?

I was still trying to work up the nerve when the door actually opened.

Commander Cullen entered and stood to one side as a man followed her into the room.

He was a big hombre, almost twice the size of the commander, dressed in watch fatigues and a hooded sweatshirt. He smiled at me. If it was supposed to be reassuring... it didn't work.

"Sr. Ellsberg," he said. "I do apologize for these circumstances—but we do have our reasons. You are welcome to either visit the baño, have more coffee, or both. Then we shall talk."

I counted the stars on the collar of the fatigues. "No offense, admiral... but should not my abrogado be present?"

"You have not been formally charged, señor—at least not yet. Pending the outcome of our talk, there may be no charges at all. If you insist upon representation in advance of this discussion, I will have to charge you. Not my preference... but you would leave me no choice."

"Admiral... I'm sorry. I didn't catch your name."

"Díaz. Hiram Díaz."

* * * *

Of course, I took both the bathroom break and the coffee under the supervision of the same portable wall of Marines that had picked me up in the first place. I play poker with a couple of lawyers, but I wouldn't consider either one of them my 'abrogado,' and I owe both of them money. Standing on my rights was going to mean at least a night in jail... maybe more.

On the other hand, I could drink some more truly awful coffee with a Navy admiral who liked to dress like a deckhand. I might even get a ride back into town. I'm not a tough guy. When someone offers me a deal, I usually take it.

The Marines escorted me back to the conference room, where Díaz and Cullen were seated on one side of the table. Next to them, something that hadn't been in the room before: a stack of file folders in official-looking navy blue jackets. The one other chair had been moved to the other side of the table and was obviously intended for me.

Díaz wasted no time once I was seated. "Sr. Ellsberg, this is potentially a simple matter. I merely need to ask you about the inspiration for one of your stories."

"As in 'where do I get my ideas'? Every Sci-Rom writer I know gets asked that question."

"Possibly not under these circumstances." The admiral removed a typed manuscript—my manuscript—from one of the folders and handed it to me. "This would be the story in question."

It was the story that had been rejected the day before. I don't always go off on a bender over a rejected story, but I'd really thought this one had some promise. "And you want to know... what, exactly?"

"The idea, Sr. Ellsberg. Where did you get the idea?"

Apparently, I was going to need that phone call after all... not that it was going to do any good.

"Admiral Díaz, here's the thing—and if this isn't good enough, you're just going to have to charge me. I literally dreamed it all up. Every single scene in that story is based on a dream."

"A dream?"

"Yes, sir... all of it."

"Do you have dreams like this often?"

"Actually, I have them all the time. It's sort of a problem."

"We may be able to help you with that."

fourteen: murphy

The second time I got to hear second-hand about 'federales' asking about 'ghost airships' was one time too many to write off. I decided to get a second opinion.

I had made camp on a low hill overlooking the desert highway. The gear I'd bought in Fort Vancouver included a portable camp stove with a windscreen. I'd made a pot of cowboy coffee, which I was spiking liberally

134

with peach brandy Maggie's parents had given me. I was wrapped in a blanket and watching the embers die in the stove. Overhead, the moonless sky was crowded with more stars than I had ever seen on any earth.

"So why are you asking me about this?" Case said. For whatever reason, he'd decided to switch out his visual avatar's wardrobe again—this time to jeans and a sherpa-lined jacket that would've made perfect sense if he'd actually been here. I was surprised he didn't include a fake cup of the same wretched spiked coffee I was drinking, but I wasn't going to bring it up.

"What's the point of having an annoying data ghost in my head if I can't ask your advice? You mostly wound up being my boss because I didn't want the job, but you were still a senior analyst for the fuckin' Company, dude. Even if I'm just imagining you, your opinion still matters."

"Gee, thanks old buddy... I think."

"You do, therefore you are. So you tell me—'ghost airships'?"

He flipped up the collar of his jacket and stared at the fire. I decided to just take the stagecraft at face value and pretend he was really there... which is probably what he really wanted. "It could be exactly what it sounds like... or not. But I agree with you that the idea of possible federal agents turning up twice in your near vicinity asking questions about UFOs is more than a little alarming. What exactly is a 'federale' under these circumstances, anyway? This isn't the United States."

"No, it's the Oregon Territory—'federale' is pretty much a blanket term for people who may or may not have badges and ask too many questions. I'm trying to keep a low profile. I didn't want to ask a lot of questions of my own, either."

"Probably a good idea."

"So what should I do about it?"

"I don't think there is very much you can do. Either someone is looking for you, or someone is looking for something... maybe 'something' that really is looking for you. Are you completely sure you were just dropped off and left?"

"As much as I'm sure of anything," I told him. "A Fortuned scoutcraft dropped me off on the Pacific coast, then re-cloaked and supposedly went back to the survey ship that brought me here—which is supposed to already be on its way back to a dimensional rift out in the Oort Cloud."

"Didn't that ever strike you as odd?"

"I was told they got out in a hurry to avoid detection and not bring this place to the attention of Greys. It fits in with everything else I was told."

Case chuckled. "That it does, old buddy—but what if what you've been told is just one big stinking pile of disinformation? We used to write this stuff for a living... are you completely sure you aren't being played?"

"Not once in my entire life, and certainly not now—not by The Obligate, and not by you. So go ahead and tell me why the people who gave me my life back are less to be trusted than a self-aware piece of viral code that just happens to look like my old boss?"

"No less, no more. They have an agenda; so do I. But my agenda includes a fairly vested interest in keeping you alive."

"I grant you that."

"I don't know everything about the people who recruited you," Case said. "I know that they've been at war with the ones that made me since before human history. I know they spun up 'The Order' the same way we spun up the Contras, only they had the idea first by a few hundred years. I don't know that they are any more 'the good guys' than the ones that made me... appearances notwithstanding."

"You've mentioned that a couple of times as well. What do you really know about Greys, Case?"

"Less than you might think, old buddy. I know they made me—although I didn't know that for a long time. I know they're why I'm good with computers and had a few other skills when I was really alive. But I know a proxy war when I see one. That's what you got recruited into; that's what I was made for."

"Do you know why Greys sent you to collect Morningstar all those years ago?"

"Not really. They didn't talk to me the way your girlfr—the way The Order spoke to you."

"Then how did you know what to do?"

"Dreams, Murphy. They talk to you in dreams."

Part 4: Armada of Ghosts

one: ellsberg

"No, Janice—I can't talk about it. The nondisclosure I signed is very specific."

I heard her sigh into the phone. "I wish you had consulted a lawyer... or maybe me." Janice wasn't a great agent, but she was pretty much the only person not holding an IOU who cared much if I lived or died. Of course, she'd called to check on me.

"Look—one of these days, when I can talk about it, I will. And let's be honest... it's not like the offers were pouring in."

"I do the best I can, Saul. Sci-Rom's a fickle market. You really should diversify."

"Don't be surprised if it gets better."

"What—the market? Or your writing?"

"Maybe both."

* * * *

I can't remember a time when I didn't have the dreams... just like I can't really remember my parents.

I remember figuring out that other people didn't dream like me—although it took a few foster parents before I learned to not talk about it. Figuring out something I could do about the dreams... was a little more complicated. Even though California Citizen Allotment covers psychic disability, the psychics in the allotment pool aren't all that great. When I was a kid, the dreams were just one problem among many.

I got older, got over some problems, and picked up some new ones. Eventually, one of my psychics suggested that I keep a journal of my dreams. So I did. At least it gave me something to do while I was waiting to stop shaking and go back to sleep.

I was working a lot of odd jobs back then, anything that I could fit around my messed-up sleep habits—janitor, cab driver, night watchman. I'd tried being a bartender; I figured out that was a bad idea. One night, on my way to some crappy job or other, I stopped at a newsstand and picked up my first Sci-Rom mag.

The stuff in the magazine wasn't any more outrageous than the stuff in my dreams. Some of it actually reminded me of my dreams. Writing helped pass the time, and it wasn't like I had much else to do that didn't involve hanging out at Harry's. As much for the heck of it as anything else, I pulled stuff from one of my old journals into a story of sorts. It wasn't all that good... but it wasn't bad, either.

And it sold.

For the first time in my life, I'd found something I was sort of good at and sort of liked doing. So I kept doing it. Being good at it made me want to be better. I took some courses, kept writing. It wasn't easy or quick, but it eventually turned into a career of sorts.

I didn't have to worry about running out of material. It turned up on a nightly basis—some of it more useful, some of it less.

Then the dreams changed, and so did my life... and not for the better.

I'd known for a long time that my dreams weren't like other people's dreams, but they were still just dreams.

Until they weren't.

* * * *

I'd never had a dream about getting arrested by military police, but I'd dreamed stranger things—and they'd seemed just as real at the time... even the ones that didn't come true.

I was sitting at a table in a conference room in a building somewhere in the East Bay Naval Preserve. I had spent the last several hours trying to imagine one good reason why I had been brought in on espionage charges. Now I knew: There wasn't one.

And I was probably going to jail... for my dreams.

Sitting across from me: the tough-looking little Navy officer who had brought me in, the admiral who'd ordered her to do it—who was now offering to 'help' me with my dreams. On the table between us: the manuscript for 'Armada of Ghosts.' It should not have been here.

Neither should I.

"What of this?" Admiral Díaz asked me. He was holding a copy of Thrilling Science Stories, the one where 'Encounter at Corona' had made cover. "Is this also from your dreams?"

I wasn't looking forward to jail, but at least I wouldn't have to worry about being late on the rent. "Yes and no. It's... complicated."

The first draft of 'Encounter at Corona' didn't even have a title; it was pretty much straight from my journal—just like most of my stuff. The second draft included... well, other material.

Sci-Rom doesn't get a lot of respect. Not everyone enjoys reading about imaginary and impossible things, the people who get to define 'literature' least of all. I'd picked up on plenty of that when I'd taken classes to improve my writing.

But whether it's literature or not, the people who do like Sci-Rom like it a lot—and its fans form a pretty tight community. For every 'real' publication like Thrilling Science Stories, there's a dozen 'fan-pubs.' If you're a published author with a mailing address, you can expect to get these things—whether you ask for them or not.

Mystery Disks Revealed wasn't particularly 'slick.' It looked like (probably was) something produced on someone's mom's office duplicator. But someone had gone to a lot of trouble to put it together, including reproducing an old Texas Air Corps press release... about an impossible thing.

The same 'impossible thing' I had dreamt of... and wrote about.

* * * *

"What is a 'fan-pub'?" Díaz asked.

"Fan publication. It's a Sci-Rom thing. Sometimes people make their own magazines."

"So, your story is actually from an amateur magazine?"

"No." Even if it meant going to jail, I was not going to be called a plagiarist. "I really did dream it and write about it. Then I got this fan-pub in the mail, and one of the things in it was a copy of what looked like an old press release. And that old press release pretty much described something from one of my dreams. I was already writing about it. I just used details from the press release to flesh it out."

"The publisher of this magazine is known to you?"

"Maybe someone I met at a Sci-Rom Con—but not personally, no."

"I should like to have this magazine," Díaz said. "Were there other issues?"

"Just the one, as far as I know—and you are welcome to it." If it kept me out of jail, he could have my entire fan-pub collection. It's not like I wouldn't get more.

* * * *

'Encounter at Corona' turned out to be the most popular thing I'd ever written. Being on the cover had probably helped—but it was obvious that I'd tapped into something a lot of people were interested in. It didn't hurt that similar stuff was starting to turn up pretty regularly in the newspapers as well.

I wondered about that sometimes. Was I having the dreams because of what was in the papers, or was it somehow the other way around? Sometimes, the dreams came first.

Before submitting the story, I'd tried to get in touch with the publisher of Mystery Disks Revealed, but the letter I sent—to a mailbox in Dallas, Texas—was returned, marked 'no such address.' Seeing things from my dreams in print, print I hadn't written, was... disturbing. I'd thought of myself as 'crazy' for years. It had been getting worse. I was either a lot less crazy than I'd thought—or maybe a lot more.

Either way, I had to know if that press release was real. I sent a letter to Texas Air Corps. I also checked the archives of San Francisco Chronicle for a month out from the date on the release. Not surprisingly, I never heard back from the Texicans. But I found what I wanted in the Chronicle.

It was buried in the back of the entertainment section and written for humorous effect, making much of Texican fondness for home-distilled corn whiskey. But it was the same story. It was the same dream.

The response to 'Encounter at Corona' was too much to ignore. By the time Thrilling Science Stories asked me for a sequel, I was already working on it.

For years, I'd been creating stories by starting out with a dream and writing a plot to go with it. With 'Armada of Ghosts,' I was going to do something a little different: write a plot, then pick dreams from my journals that fit into the plot. I'll be the first to admit the plot wasn't entirely original. Invaders from other worlds is a trope older than literature.

On the other hand, my dreams are entirely mine, and I had plenty to pick from. They'd been becoming more frequent and intense for months. Mixed in with dreams of fantastic things that might be true were dreams of very ordinary things that sometimes did come true. I had stopped seeing psychists. I knew they couldn't help.

The only thing that did help, other than drinking, was writing. And for once, I'd actually known what I wanted to write about.

* * * *

When Díaz had first entered the room, a pair of antique specs had been perched atop his head. He was now peering through them as he shuffled through the stack of file jackets that had been brought in during my bathroom break. Toward the bottom of the stack, he apparently found what he was looking for—two jackets, which he placed in front of me. Unlike the rest of the stack, which were all marked 'Top Secret,' these were just stamped 'Confidential—RCN Access Only.'

After a brief search of his pockets, the admiral found a pen and placed it next to the files. "Sr. Ellsberg, there is a possibility that we may be able to help each other. But first I need a decision from you.

"This," he pointed to the first file jacket, "is a fairly standard confidentiality agreement required of all civilian contractors who handle sensitive information. I will need your signature on this before I can discuss anything else with you in detail. Sign it, and the current charges against you can be dropped.

"This," he pointed to the second file jacket, "is an offer of employment—a consulting agreement between yourself and BSI. It is an exclusive arrangement under which you would suspend your activities as a freelance writer as part of a long-term contract assignment.

"The details of this assignment are also confidential. You would be well compensated. You would also be offered therapeutic options for these dreams of yours, as well as... other assistance, which is also confidential. You are under no obligation to take this offer—but if you wish to know more, I need you to first sign the confidentiality agreement—after which we may, should you like, discuss an offer of employment. If you are not interested in this offer, you are free to leave."

The admiral looked at me over the tops of his glasses. He was no longer smiling. "This will not be so if you do not sign the agreement. In that case, we must proceed with formal charges. You will remain under custody until you are formally arraigned. There will, of course, be no further proceedings until your legal counsel is present.

"Do you have any questions, señor?"

I looked at the folders for a long time. I could sign the agreement, turn down the job offer, and walk out the door... apparently a free man, if I could take it at face value the guy who'd had me arrested in the first place. Or I could hang tough and insist on an abrogado who couldn't do much more than help me get out of jail sooner rather than later.

At which point I would get to add legal fees to the stack of unpaid bills and rejection letters sitting back at my apartment.

I unclasped the first file jacket. I have no idea what a 'standard' confidentiality agreement would look like, but this seemed straightforward. Agreeing to keep state secrets I didn't really know in the first place was no big deal—particularly if the alternative meant going to jail. I read it again, then signed it. "This means I'm free to go?"

"If you like," Admiral Díaz said. "This meeting and everything we have discussed is confidential and not to be disclosed. As far as concerns the public, none of this has happened. Certainly, you may leave—but you are also now free to examine the offer we have prepared for you. You need not answer at this time, but this as well is confidential—you may examine the offer, but it does not leave this room."

I wasn't sure how 'real' any of this was, but given the way my head hurt, I was pretty sure it wasn't a dream. And a job might be nice... real or not.

I opened the second jacket. The yearly salary offer was roughly equal to every penny I'd made in the last ten years. The job description read 'technical writer and research assistant, assignment details TBD.'

I looked at the offer amount again. I realized that those 'TBD' details were no importante. I was pretty sure this was not what my agent had in mind when she'd suggested I try something besides writing Sci-Rom... but it was also a lot better than anything she'd managed to turn up.

"So, when do I start?"

"You wish to accept? Next week, I should think," Díaz said. "We'll need to set up an office for you, as well as a few other administrative details."

"You really think you can help me with my dreams? I didn't see anything about that."

Díaz shrugged. "That is among the 'to be determined' details we are still working on. At the very least, Navy psychists are better than those in Citizen Allotment. Your dreams are not what you think, Sr. Ellsberg—they are not what anyone thinks."

"Then... I'm not imagining it?"

"Imagining what, Señor?" It was even harder to say it aloud than it had been to think about it. "I dream impossible things," I said. "And sometimes, those things come true."

two: kayce

I'd grown up the daughter of a respected academic... who had a fondness for trash fiction, which he also enjoyed writing. By the time it was common knowledge that Professor Elliot Parkes-Cullen was also 'Clarke Kimball,' it would take more than writing a book like Scourge of the Aether Patrol to damage Pops's reputation, much less my respect for him.

But it still took some getting used to.

"You know these sci-rom types are all crazy, right?"

"I don't know anything of the kind," Pops retorted. "And the last time I checked, I'm one of them—am I 'crazy,' darlin'?'

I was as likely to win the argument as I was the chess game, but I was young and sure of myself. We were sitting in Pops' study. I had just gotten home from my first tour.

"All they do is talk about impossible things. And you aren't really 'one of them.' Knight to King's Four."

"Oh, but I am," he chuckled, moving a pawn to block my knight. "As for 'impossible things,' you just spent the better part of two years traveling around the Pacific on the taxpayer's dime. If you learned so little from it that you think you know for a fact everything that's 'possible'... I think perhaps the taxpayers deserve a refund."

If I hadn't decided to go into the Navy, I could've wound up just like Pops. We're a lot alike. We both have a passion for history, we're both short and blond, both attracted to women taller and darker than ourselves. Looking across the chessboard was like looking into a mirror of a possible future— longer and more silver hair, contacts given up for glasses, the eyes behind the glasses the same blue as mine.

I would probably wind up better dressed, though; it is most unlikely that my Esmerelda would permit me to wear anything as ratty as Pops's old sweater and worn chinos, even at home. Lucky for me, I look good in blue and can let the Navy make my wardrobe choices for me. "If all the taxpayers are getting for their pesos is my 'education,' Pops, they absolutely deserve a refund." I looked down at the board and saw an opening. "Queen to Queen's Seven."

"Interesting," Pops said. "Maybe you learned something after all."

"I learned that the world's a big place. And you're right: I saw things on my last tour that I probably never would've believed if I hadn't seen them with my own eyes. But I still know what's possible and what isn't—and I think a lot of your Sci-Rom buddies aren't completely clear on the concept."

Pops stared at the chessboard for a long time—deep in thought or deep in strategy, or maybe both. Finally, he spoke. "A fair number of my 'Sci-Rom buddies' include folks who do science for a living—including a few over in the Physics department, who have theories that make your distinction between 'possible' and 'impossible' almost meaningless. If they are even halfway right, the world we see is just part of a bigger world where everything is possible... and an 'impossibility' is just a possibility you haven't met yet—oh, and by the way," he moved a piece. "Check. Mate in three moves."

I'm not a bad player, but Pops is one of the best. And it turned out he was right about the possibility of meeting impossible things... even impossible people.

* * * *

I hadn't known I was arresting Saul Ellsberg so Hiram Díaz could offer him a job until shortly after it happened. "Technically, he's not a technical writer," I said.

"And not really qualified as a research assistant," the admiral replied. "I had to put down something to get Human Resources to approve the contract."

"I'm surprised they approved the salary."

The admiral shrugged. "It's well within our discretionary budget."

"Do you think he'll agree to it?" We were sitting in the admiral's office. I could see Saul Ellsberg fidgeting on a televisor. Likely as not, the poor man needed to visit the baño. "Pulling a man out of bed at gunpoint isn't known to be an exceptional recruiting tool."

"You haven't done fieldwork, Kayce—sometimes it works wonders. In any case, I do not care. I had you bring in Sr. Ellsberg to impress upon him the importance of this confidentiality agreement. I don't particularly wish to see this man in San Quentin—but if he continues to write of things every government in North America wishes kept secret... that is where he is going."

If this was what my new assignment called for, I wasn't sure I wanted it. Being a history professor was beginning to sound awfully good. I sighed. "Just tell me what you need me to do, sir."

"Very little, for now. I will do the talking with Sr. Ellsberg. If he agrees to my offer, he will be working under your direction. If he declines the offer, I will need you to monitor his compliance with the confidentiality agreement."

"And if he does not sign the agreement?"

Díaz looked up at Ellsberg's image in the monitor. I couldn't tell if he saw an obstacle, an opportunity, or a threat... but I knew that he would see nothing else. "Only a very brave or very stupid man would do such a thing, and I do not believe this man either particularly brave... or particularly stupid."

* * * *

The great man was right. He usually is. One of these days, I will stop being annoyed by it.

Saul Ellsberg had signed the confidentiality papers almost immediately. The admiral might have expected a similar result with the offer letter; might not have cared one way or the other. But that's not what happened.

"… impossible things," Ellsberg said. "And sometimes, those things come true. It's real, isn't it?"

I hadn't expected Saul Ellsberg to tell us he'd literally dreamed up a story he was in custody for writing, much less that Admiral Díaz might actually believe him. But then, I hadn't expected to be told that 'ghost airships' and 'mystery disks' were real… or that they occasionally crashed in Texas.

I had worked in BSI long enough to know better than to take anything at face value—most particularly anything having to do with Hiram Díaz. He was as smart as Pops and played people the way Pops played chess pieces—ruthlessly, with layers of strategy. Unlike Pops, the admiral's preferred game was poker… when he could get up a game, that is. Whether he actually believed Saul Ellsberg or not was more than I could say. There could be any number of reasons he was offering the man a job, reasons he might or might not share with me… which might or might not be damned lies if he did.

"The question of what is 'real' in any large sense is not one I can answer, Sr. Ellsberg," the admiral said. "Although I can assure you that the assignment you are being offered is, indeed, quite real. As concerns your dreams… let us just say that I have reasons to not dismiss what you are saying, reasons I am not at liberty to share. Speculate privately on these reasons as you like. Speculate publicly, and you will again be facing possible incarceration.

"Should you wish to accept this job, the possibility exists that you may be granted elevated security clearances that would permit me to share more. But I cannot promise this. And I can offer no assurance that what you suspect of your dreams is any more or less 'real' than anything else."

"At least you aren't just telling me I'm crazy," Ellsberg said with a bitter laugh. "Is there anything else you can tell me at all?"

"Beyond what is in that letter? I offer my assurance that the work you would contribute to is a matter of the highest importance, that you would be well-treated as a member of my team, and that whatever answers we are able to find, we will share with you as much as we can. Again, I do not need an immediate answer."

Ellsberg looked over the offer letter again, laughing again as he signed it. "I'm probably just dreaming this, anyway."

three: murphy

Most of the 'magic' I'd been exposed to as part of The Order had been of the 'Clarke's Third Law' variety... but not all of it. I know a few things and know how to do a few things. Like most with such abilities, I really don't know how it works—just that it does. Generally, I prefer technology over magic. It's more reliable. You summon a demon, and neither you or the demon really know how it's going to turn out.

I've participated in an exorcism or two. While I could probably banish the data ghost living in my head, it was also entirely possible that I could damage some highly sophisticated technology, thousands of years more advanced than anything else I had ever seen... which was also in my head.

As long as I could turn Case off when I felt like it, I was inclined to leave well enough alone. He was useful, and I was beginning to remember why I'd ever liked the guy in the first place. Taking on the appearance of the kid who'd been my favorite wingman back in the day probably helped.

I was deep into the desert under a merciless steel blue sky, watching the miles scroll by and feeling my old life and my old self recede into more than cosmic distance.

It wasn't just that I had been made young again. Elixir Vitae had rewritten me from the source code out. I no longer knew who or what I really was.

Truth be told, the old me had hardly been worth preserving. He was a bitterly lonely old man who'd made mistakes for which he blamed himself long after anyone else who'd been involved had either forgiven, forgotten... or just died. What Evangeia had ever seen in him beyond usefulness was a question that might get answered if we found ourselves again in the same universe. That I had at least been useful enough to be 'preserved' was at least of use to me... and would have to do for now.

* * * *

I don't even know the name of the town. Road signage was even more hit-or-miss than pavement on the highways that crossed the continent's backbone... and were only nominally owned by anyone. Only the poor or dispossessed traveled this way—as well, sometimes, those preferring to attract as little attention to themselves as possible.

Like me.

I had considered riding at night to avoid the furnace heat of day until I saw the state of the roads I would be traveling, which got steadily worse further south. I'd made a point of refueling every chance I'd had. I carried extra fuel as well in the sidecar. I could see why Carl had been so impressed with the Armstrong. It was an ugly, tough, capable machine that had been designed for rough conditions. The kid had done an impressive job restoring it. Maybe someday, I'd sell it back to him. Or maybe just give it to him.

After two days' travel across a barren wasteland that just called itself 'America,' I found myself in a town that might as well have had no name... not one I would've known in any case.

Neon signs had also been discovered in this world, put to the same usage... human nature being what it was. In front of me was an adobe and sheet metal building with windows fairly thick with the stuff.

A beer sounded like a really good idea... human nature being what it was.

There was an assortment of other bikes, trikes, and four-wheelers in the parking lot. It seemed not unlikely that their owners might have other similarities with myself... which might or might not be a good thing.

At least the interior was air-conditioned. Not as ubiquitous as it was on my world, but they had it where it mattered. I bellied up to the bar. "Whatever's cold," I said, throwing down some coins.

"Oh, it's all cold, son," the bartender replied. "But I ain't taking no Californy money."

"Apologies," I said. "Didn't realize it was an issue. Here's a John Quincy— round up, keep a buck."

"That works," the bartender said, handing me a beer and some change. "Cheers."

"Back at ya."

The beer was bottled, cold as advertised. Not as good as what I'd gotten used to in the Northwest, but it did the trick.

I was considering another when the space next to me acquired an occupant. He was a big guy and probably would've had a red face even if he didn't have the chronic sunburn of white guys that don't know to stay out of the sun. The straw hat had a wider brim and a rounder crown than the ones I remembered, but the boots, belt, and jeans were pretty much the same.

"That RCN Marine scout's a nice rig... yours?"

"It is. Thanks."

"Sure. Word to the wise, son—don't be payin' for drinks with pesos 'round here."

"Didn't think it was a problem." Strictly speaking, it wasn't. They even called it the 'North American Free Trade Agreement,' though it was older and had different provisions. There was a one-to-one exchange rate guaranteed between U.S. Dollars and California Pesos. It got balanced out at the backend by the banks and paid for in taxes. Every once in a while, someone floated the idea of a common currency, but no one expected 'Ameros' any time soon.

"Well, it is—we're Americans 'round these parts."

I wasn't sure where this was going; pretty sure I didn't give a shit. "Thanks for the advice."

"No problem. So, where ya headed?"

"Galveston, more or less."

"Where ya from?"

"Started in Astoria... more or less."

"Kinds short on details, son. You got a name?"

"Name's Murphy. And you are...?"

"Johnson. Lew Johnson. Interestin' jacket," he said, eyeing my leathers. "That the style back where you're from?"

"I don't think it's been a 'style' anywhere for a while... but it comes in handy."

"I reckon so. Looks old—you get it from your daddy?"

"You could call him that," I said.

Johnson sniggered. "Leastways he left you somethin.' All my daddy left behind was a stack of IOUs."

"The man I got this from left a few of those as well," I said. "They're mine now, too." I finished my beer. "Pleased to meet you, Mr. Johnson. Good talking to ya, but I got a long ways to go."

"Actually, you don't, son. It's 'Sheriff' Johnson, not 'Mister Johnson'—and you ain't goin' no place."

four: ellsberg

Even though the California Civil Liberties Union would probably consider me a victim, and half the communards in Berkeley would condemn me as a tool of the military-industrial complex, I wasn't feeling all that victimized... or used.

After I'd signed the offer letter, Admiral Díaz shook my hand. "I again apologize for the manner in which you were brought here, but not the necessity of it. Perhaps this will help make amends."

He searched his stack of file jackets, found what he was looking for, handed me a check. "Under the terms of our agreement, BSI has an option to purchase as many of your unpublished manuscripts as we wish. I

155

should like to purchase them all. I believe the amount of this check is sufficient to that end. Do you agree?"

I did. Someone had gone to the trouble of adding up every single debt I had and rounded up to the next even thousand. And in another two weeks, I would be receiving a paycheck as well. "Just make sure my agent receives her customary commission," I said.

"Consider it done," Díaz said. "Is it safe to assume that we can include in this transaction your collection of amateur publications as well?"

"Absolutely," I told him. "Is there anything else?"

"Two things, actually, but they are small. First, it is my understanding that you have a number of journals detailing these dreams of yours. The... therapy we are hoping to offer would proceed more quickly if these journals could be included in this transaction."

"Done," I told him. Like the fanzines, there was plenty more where that came from.

"Second, you receive amateur publications like Mystery Disks Revealed with some frequency, yes?"

"Fan-pubs, yes. Like that one? Not so much."

"I understand the distinction. My interest is not in self-published scientific romances. But if you receive anything else like that one, I wish to be informed."

* * * *

I wound up riding back to my apartment in what looked like the same staff car that brought me in. There was just one marine this time, who collected me from Díaz's office once the admiral was done with me and who was now sitting in front with the driver.

I polished off what was left of my Two Peso Chuck as soon as I made it home. I'd thought about hitting Harry's as well, decided against it. Until I was a lot clearer on what I was and was not supposed to be talking about, drinking at home seemed like a good idea. If it wasn't for the large stack of documents I had been given to sign and bring back, I could have easily woke up the next day, convinced none of it had really happened... that it was just another dream.

I've lived in San Francisco all my life, known plenty of people who wound up working for the government. I hadn't known that many people who'd had BSI show up at their door with a warrant... but it wasn't unheard of.

San Francisco is the actual capital of California, the unofficial capital of the PNW Federation, and home base for the California Navy. There's no shortage in this town of secrets bought and sold... I had just never thought of myself as being in the market.

It was closer to two weeks later that I finally caught the morning commute train across the Bay and reported for work. It had been a long, long time since 'work' had meant anything to me besides rolling out of bed, putting on coffee, and staring at a typewriter until the words started happening. It had never been anything like this. But the money was good... and it beat going to jail.

I'd been told to check in at the reception desk when I arrived at BSI. A few minutes after I did, Mathilde Juarez popped out of the lift to collect me, cheerful as always. "Hola, Saul. Any trouble getting here?"

"It was fine, Mathilde."

Mathilde showed me how to use my new security badge to get to the lift. I was able to figure out how to badge in on my own when we got to the floor where I'd be working. "We managed to find space for you next to Commander Cullen by converting a file room. The admiral and I are two floors up—but I guess you remember that."

"Not really. I'm not a morning person, and I had just gotten arrested. But I'll remember it now."

It was pretty easy to tell that the office was a converted file closet, but I'm not particularly claustrophobic... although I do have other phobias.

"Navy Net-Terms aren't exactly like civilian ones," Mathilde said, pointing to the object that took up most of my desk. "I'm probably going to have to show you a few things before you can use it."

"Actually, you may have to show me more than you think," I told her. "I don't own a 'net terminal. I write on a typewriter."

The cheerful expression went away for a moment—but just a moment. Then she reached over to the phone on my desk. "Nancy," she said. "Could you please take my calls for a bit? Something just came up. I'm probably going to be busy for a while."

* * * *

I had gotten a fair amount of grief over the years for being slow to embrace the 'Net Revolution.' Sci-Rom writers are expected to obsess with technology. The younger ones pretty much do. But I'd found out I loved to write banging away on an old used typewriter I'd gotten on the cheap in a thrift store.

I wasn't going to catch up in a single day on technology I'd been ignoring for the better part of twenty years, but with Mathilde's help, I reached the point where I could at least read and respond to my 'net messages and find my way around the parts of RCN and BSI's private networks they were going to let me see.

"You're lucky you're working for the admiral," Mathilde told me. "He doesn't really like technology either."

"Then he's lucky to have an office administrator like you," I said.

"More than you know, Saul... more than you know."

The rest of the day was spent filling out more forms, reading manuals, finding out what I was permitted to do, finding out what I could do that would get me in jail after all. There was a lot of that.

Mid-afternoon Kayce Cullen showed up, looking much as she had when she'd arrested me—minus the portable wall of marines and the disapproving schoolteacher expression. "The admiral asked me to check in on you. Everything okay?"

"Truthfully, I'm a little overwhelmed, Commander. It might've been simpler if I'd just been charged with espionage."

"Nothing is 'simple' if Hiram Díaz is involved," she replied. "And you can just call me 'Kayce.' The admiral runs an informal shop."

Call me 'Kayce.' Something that had been floating around in the back of my mind for at least a week finally clicked. "I just realized," I told her. "You're Kayce Cullen-Figueroa. I know your father."

She smiled. "I'm just 'Commander Cullen' while we're on base. The Navy's a little conservative and I don't really use my married name. But, yeah—that's me. How do you know Pops?"

"We were on a panel together at the Fresno Sci-Rom Con last year. We didn't talk that much, but I know he's very proud of you."

"I'm pretty proud of him, even though I'm not that fond of his writing hobby—no offense."

I shrugged. "None taken, Commander. Anyone who writes Sci-Rom who isn't your pops is pretty used to not being taken seriously."

"Why do it?" she asked.

"You do it because you love it, or you do it because you have to... pretty much like anything else. In my case, a little of both."

"Fair enough. Any questions so far?"

"Lots of little ones, one big one—the one I've been asking ever since you arrested me: why am I here?

"All of this," I waved my hand over the pile of manuals and forms taking up what little desk space was left from the 'net terminal, "just tells me how to work for Navy Intelligence and not wind up in San Quentin. Don't get me wrong—I appreciate the job, really appreciate that I'm not in San Quentin already. But I still don't understand what you and the admiral actually expect I'm going to do."

Kayce looked at her watch. "There's a pretty good cafe next door in the admin tower. I usually nip over for a latte about this time of day... or if I'm feeling a little 'overwhelmed.' Let's go have a coffee. My treat."

five: murphy

I'd had a bad feeling from the moment 'Sheriff Johnson' sat down.

While he was clarifying his introduction, he reached for my sidearm. There are a couple of ways to arrest someone in a place where everyone's carrying. He'd picked the one that's usually safer.

Usually.

The bartender produced a double-barreled sawed-off from behind the bar. Behind me, I heard what sounded like Sheriff Johnson's backup moving into place. They should've gone with one or the other. But it still would've worked if my sidearm had left the holster like it was supposed to.

But I knew that wasn't going to happen.

In the moment when Johnson expected to take my gun, something else happened instead. I lunged forward and right, grabbed the shotgun, rammed it hard enough against the bar to discharge both barrels into the space where I'd been the moment before—as well as into whoever had been moving into place behind me.

Ripping the shotgun from the bartender with my left hand, I slammed the stock upward into his face, back-handing Johnson—who was still trying to unholster my weapon—at the same time with my right.

I spun and then wound up with my back to the bar, striking the bartender with the shotgun again to ensure he would stay down. The fake service revolver came away from the holster into my own hand—as I knew it would.

The sheriff was sprawled on his back on the floor and reaching for his own weapon. I fired first. He went down just as fast as anyone else, shot point-blank in the face. The shot rang out just as loud—but his head was still intact. 'Non-lethal setting.' He'd actually live to work on his arrest tactics.

The space between me and the exit was empty, except for the deputy or whatever the fuck who'd tried to get behind me. He was actually in worse shape than the sheriff was, but that wasn't my problem. Everyone else in the room was sitting very still with their hands where I could see them. Good.

I kept the shotgun as a prop as I made my way around the guy I'd used it on. It was useless, but anyone who might be on the other side of the door wouldn't necessarily know that.

There was only one other vehicle in the parking lot that hadn't been there when I went in—no official markings, not that I'd know what to look for— and no other people.
I slung the shotgun into the street and mounted the Armstrong. Twenty minutes later and ten miles up the road, the shakes hit, and I found myself badly in need of a cigarette or cigarette equivalent. I settled for a swig of the peach brandy I'd carried with me out of Oregon.

Too many questions, too few answers. The man I'd once been had bequeathed to the man I'd become a leather jacket, an Obligation or two, and the mystery of just who or what the hell I really was.

I wondered what I would see the next time I looked in the mirror.

six: kayce

It was going to take more than a coffee break to answer Saul's questions. I couldn't share everything I knew—and I was myself operating on a 'need to know' basis.
The admiral had made that very clear.

If the thing that crashed in 1947 had crashed in California, it would've been better for just about everyone. Well, not for the things onboard the thing. They'd be just as dead. But the United States wouldn't have physical possession of an artifact from elsewhere, and the Republic of California wouldn't have to share advanced technology with a country known for making bad choices... that were apparently getting worse.

Had the thing crashed in the U.S. proper, the Majestic partnership likely might not have happened at all—at the very least, it could have been decades before the U.S. had to admit they needed help. But because the Texas Air Corps is about as much a real military as Texas is a real republic, the whole thing wound up in the papers before it could be contained. The joint coverup operation escalated into Majestic.

And now Majestic was escalating into yet something else.

"If it is a threat, Kayce, it is a threat like no other. Things appear in the sky—more daily—of no known human agency, behaving in ways that contradict all known human experience. But assessing and analyzing threats is what we do—even this one. To assess the impossible, one must accept the merely unlikely."

Four days after Saul Ellsberg's 'recruitment,' I had again been called to Admiral Díaz's office. I was going to be told what I needed to know in order to supervise my new 'research assistant'... or at least what the admiral thought I needed to know.

"Admiral, you put a pulp fiction writer on payroll after he told us he was literally dreaming up the stuff up you had me bring him in for writing. This happened the day after you upped my security clearance so you could tell me 'mystery disks' are real. If this is some sort of test, I hope I passed it."

Díaz chuckled. "It is no test, but you have passed anyway—you always do. That is why you are here. You are among our best and brightest, Kayce. Were you to choose a command career path, you would go far."

I'd heard that before, more times than I care to think about. For a moment, I considered trying to explain to a straight man from a privileged family why I had to be 'the best and brightest'—but only for a moment. I could more easily believe mystery disks were real than I could imagine any good coming from that conversation.

"I suppose it's still an option," I said. "But I like teaching. And the Bureau is an interesting place to work."

"Even though you continue to doubt the reality of your current assignment?"

"Most people would, Admiral."

"'Most people' do not see the things we see, Kayce. This, for example." He held up a crudely printed 'magazine' in a sealed forensics lab wrapper. The title: Mystery Disks Revealed.

"That's the—what did he call it? 'Fan-pub'?"

"Correct. Short for 'fan publication.' Under our agreement with Sr. Ellsberg, we now have a large collection of these things—the actual value of which, with this one exception, is a very small fraction of what was paid for it."

"How is this exceptional?" I asked. "It looks like something someone ran off on an office copier."

"Appearances can be deceiving, as we both know all too well. However this was made, it was not merely 'run off on an office copier'—although someone went to great lengths to make it seem that way.

"The analysis I requested is not complete, but this 'fan-pub' appears to have been fabricated in ways similar to advanced computer-guided micro-fabrication techniques—I believe the emerging term for it is '3D printing.' Be assured this thing did not come from Texas, regardless the supposed publisher's address. This information is not to be shared with Sr. Ellsberg, by the way—or our Yanqui counterparts, should the situation arise."

"Understood, sir."

"Neither Sr. Ellsberg nor his dreams are what they seem. I am not disposed to discuss all of this—even a gold-alpha level security clearance has 'need to know' limitations. For the time being, indulge me. You will be conducting research of your own, as well as supervising Ellsberg."

"What sort of research, sir?"

"You are a historian, among other things, Kayce. Ellsberg suggests in his stories that the crashed artifact the Yanquis have in their possession comes from the same source as these other things from a century before, these so-called 'ghost airships.' What if that is true? Try to think of this both as a military analyst as well as a historian."

Lucky for the admiral, I'm both those things, as well as the daughter of another historian who also likes to write—and talk about—Sci-Rom. I'd had conversations like this before; I just never thought I'd be taking one seriously... or that the other participant would not be Pops but Hiram Díaz.

"It could mean a lot of things, Admiral. It would mean that whatever is behind this is planning on a timeline that extends over decades, if not centuries. As to what that plan actually is, we can't really say. Maybe it's an 'invasion,' maybe something else. Something that evolved on another planet is no more likely to think like us than it would look like. Their intentions may not make sense in human terms at all."

"Very good—continue."

"It could also mean there might be other such crashed artifacts as well, yet to be found, that didn't conveniently crash where they could be recovered by the Texas Air Corps."

"Quite possibly. Any other thoughts?"

"Just one, Admiral," I replied. "If we're talking about a nonhuman presence that has been here for at least a century, perhaps they have been here even longer. And if these things, whatever they are, have been here for decades or centuries, how do we know they don't have allies by now?"

"You mean human allies?" the admiral asked. "Here and now?"

"It would certainly be possible."

"All of this is implied, and more—and that is the nature of the research you will be conducting. It is something for which you are uniquely qualified. Given recent events, it is something I feel very strongly we should do. I am more certain than ever that placing 'Project Ikelos' in your hands was the right decision."

"'Project Ikelos'?"

"You may read into the name whatever you like. It is not inappropriate, given the project brief.

"Now, as to Sr. Ellsberg: until you receive other instructions, take the matter of his dreams entirely at face value. It is clear that parties unknown have gone to some lengths to ensure that these dreams wind up in print. We are going to find out why."

"'Parties unknown,' sir?"

"Certainly for now, commander."

* * * *

"That's it?" Saul said.

The cafe was a nice change from Saul Ellsberg's converted file room 'office.' It was tucked into a corner of the RCN admin tower—next to the commissary, with a nice view of the bay. The coffee was an even nicer change. I'd gotten my usual latte, bought Saul an Americano, then steered him to a back table where we could talk.

"That's really it," I told him. "Read the reports, analyze them. If you see anything you recognize, note it in your own reports."

"Recognize? You mean from Sci-Rom?"

"Or from your dreams." Díaz had given me my orders; I was going to follow them. "Your contract is intentionally open, when it comes to your job description. For now, you're a 'research assistant.' The admiral thinks you have, or have access to, information he wants. He's willing to pay to get it. It's information he wants to control. He's paying for that as well."

Saul had shown up for work in the same suit he'd worn the day I'd taken him in, now with a pressed shirt and a tie. He still had a face like a sad and somewhat confused basset hound. It shouldn't surprise me he knew Pops. It shouldn't even matter... but it did. Whatever Hiram Díaz was up to, Saul Ellsberg would receive no further mistreatment if I could possibly help it.

He sipped his coffee and looked out across the bay. "Am I ever going to know what this is really about?"

"The admiral thinks you already do, somehow. We're trying to figure that out."

"Is it okay to ask what you're doing?"

"You can always ask, Saul. Ask me anything you want, ask Mathilde. If you think it's really important, ask Admiral Díaz—although I highly recommend that you ask me first. Just don't take it personally if the answer from any of us is 'I can't tell you that.'"

"So, 'what are you doing, Kayce?'"

"I can't tell you that." I held a serious expression as long as I could, then laughed. "Sorry, Saul—I can never quite pass on a straight line."

He smiled back, seeming less sad for a moment. "No surprise there. Your pops is the same way."

"He's worse, really," I replied. "What I can tell you is that I'm reading the same reports you are and also analyzing them—from the perspective of my own specialty.

"You're a professor of military and strategic history. What on earth does that have in common with Sci-Rom... or my dreams?"

"Maybe nothing 'on earth'... and in any case, that's something I really can't tell you. I understand if you find any of this frustrating. More than any other part of the Navy, BSI operates on a 'need to know' basis. You've been told what you need to know to do the job you've been hired to do, and my situation isn't very different—until very recently, all I knew about any of this was what I read in the papers."

"Do you believe me?" he asked. The smile had passed. He wasn't just sad. He was haunted. Whatever he experienced in his dreams was very much not something I 'needed to know.'

I would have to choose my words carefully. "One of the smartest and most ruthlessly practical men I have ever met either believes you, or has what he considers a good reason to treat your story as true. He's also promised to share that good reason, however soon and however much he can. He's also promised you'll be well-treated. You have the same promise from me."

He smiled again, even though the eyes remained sad. "I even believe it in your case, Kayce."

"But not the admiral?"

"I looked him up as soon as I had a chance," Saul said. "Or let's just say I tried to. Your admiral has a remarkably low public profile. He runs BSI, doesn't he?"

"I'm not at liberty to add much to whatever you found in a public library or online. But I can tell you that I trust him... and I think you can as well. I'm sorry, by the way."

"Sorry?"

"Sorry for arresting you. The admiral apologized. I should as well."

The sadness left Saul's eyes, and he laughed. "Oh, no apology needed, Kayce. You were doing your job—and now I have one, too. One of these days, when it won't get you court-martialed, I'd love for you to give my regards to your Pops. Meanwhile, thanks for the coffee."

seven: murphy

Despite the crappy quality of the roads, I drove through the night and into the next day after the incident with Sheriff Johnson, wanting as many miles behind me as possible. The attempted confiscation of my ride had occurred at a highway crossroad, and decided my mind in favor of a detour I'd been considering, anyway.

Even though the new and improved me had refined combat skills and enough stamina to drive a motorcycle almost twenty-four hours straight, I still had my limits. By the time the sun was again lowering in the sky, I realized
I would soon need to stop. I found a likely spot not far off the highway. I was setting up camp when I noticed a derelict building on a nearby hill. There wasn't much of a road to it, but it looked passable. I threw everything back in the sidecar and relocated for the night.

The abandoned adobe ruin had either been a ranch, or farm house, or a barn, or a combination of all three. All that really remained were three standing walls, the remains of a fourth, and a few roof timbers. It would offer no protection from the elements, but it did offer concealment and a view. I would know about anyone else on the highway long before they knew anything about me.

I found enough brush to fuel my camp stove, picked out the least offensive of my diminishing supply of freeze-dried crap, soon had what passed for a meal. To say that I was getting tired of my own 'cooking' would be a massive understatement.

* * * *

"I miss all the fun," Case said. "Would it kill you to leave the social interface switched on once in a while?"

"Actually, it might." I replied. "I don't need to be distracted by a cheering section when I'm trying to not get arrested or shot."

I had decided it would be a good idea to check in with the talking computer virus in my head. Even though I was at least somewhat talking to myself, he was the data ghost of a fairly smart guy, and I was beginning to find his advice useful.

I heard a ghostly, dry chuckle in my head. "It sounds like you were doing all the shooting. Are you planning to go into full ninja mode every time some small-town cop asks to see your license? I thought you were supposed to keep a low profile?"

"This guy wasn't exactly asking and may not exactly have been a cop. It happened pretty fast, and I kind of reacted on instinct."

"Have you always had instincts like that?"

"Not really... and that's one of the things I wanted to ask you about."

Case 'walked' over to the edge of the ruined wall and looked out into the deepening twilight. Once again, I found myself wondering what he really saw. "Ask away," he said.

"For starters—what the hell are you looking at?"

"Pretty much whatever you're looking at. The nanotech they put in your eyes can pick up what you see as well as plant things in your vision. Whatever your implants can access, I can access as well."

"Any particular reason you look like the 'you' I met 30 years ago?"

He shrugged. "It's fun. You like this instead?" There was a staticky blur across my vision as he morphed into the mutated thing I'd seen in a tank in Greenland.

I shuddered. "Not really. I think you have the right idea." Another staticky blur, and 'Club Kid Case' was back, still rocking location-appropriate jeans and jacket.

"So," he said. "What else, old buddy?"

"Whatever you know about the tech I'm carrying around in my head, I need to know. They didn't just rejuvenate me, Case. I also need a second opinion on what just happened."

"Let's start with that. I'm going to guess you're trying to figure out whether you just shot a cop in the face or some rando bandito claiming to be a cop."

"Something like that."

"You didn't make any friends by not killing him, by the way. It may be 'non-lethal,' but that shit hurts like a motherfucker—at least it did that time you did the same thing to me. Did he show any kind of badge or identification?"

"Not really. He said he was a sheriff and went for my gun. Thirty seconds later, he was on the floor, and I was out the door."

"Still wish I'd gotten to see it," Case said. "Really, there's just three options: either he wasn't a real cop, he was a real cop who wanted your stuff, or... it was what you're worried about."

"I thought you couldn't read my mind?"

"I can't, I don't need to—we were both trained by the same professional paranoids. I may not have your field experience, but I sent plenty of people out there... and they didn't all come back.

"Twice, you've had people tell you you'd just missed 'federales' who may or may not have been looking for you and were also asking questions about 'ghost airships.' This world may not be as wired as ours, but it's wired enough—wired enough that Sheriff Cletus or whatever his name was could've been acting on a 'person of interest' bulletin... or whatever they call them here."

It didn't matter whether I was talking to myself, interacting with a piece of viral code, or having an actual conversation with what practically amounted to a ghost. Whatever it was, it was confirming my own fears.

"In other words," I said, "things could get pretty interesting once I'm out of this fucking desert. To the tune of a roadblock, or maybe getting busted by a more real and/or less stupid cop."

"Could be, old buddy... could be. It might be a good idea to—hey, what's that?"

"What's what?"

"Turn your head back where it just was. Tell me what you see."

Slowly, I turned my head back.

"There," he said. "Do you see that?"

"I thought you could only see what I see."

"I do—including the stuff you don't notice. One of the reasons you might consider leaving me switched on more often. You see it now... don't you?"

"I do. What the hell?" There was a light in the sky to the north, apparently following the highway. There were aircraft in this world... but not like this. A cluster of brightly colored pinpoints around a larger point that appeared white was drifting toward us. As it got closer, I could see another cluster behind the first. As it got even closer, I got a sense of scale: it was big.

Closer still, and I could tell that the clusters of light were at either end of a flattened cylinder that drew to a point at either end. The only other light available was starlight, but that was enough for my implants. I could tell it was metallic, and smooth.

Even closer. It had to be at least the length of a football field. It passed over the place I'd earlier thought to make camp. A beam like a spotlight speared down from one of the white lights, illuminating the place I'd been.

Then it went out.

Continuing to follow the highway, it passed within yards of our hillside ruin. In the starlight, my enhanced vision could make out elaborate tracing etched into the metal, like Celtic knotwork.

Then it passed, moving onward to the south, once again diminishing to pinpoints in the star-filled desert sky.

Finally, Case broke the silence in my mind. "'What the hell?' Actually, I have no idea, old buddy. That's a new one on me."

eight: ellsberg

On the second day of my 'job,' I arrived to find a stack of reports I was supposed to analyze sitting on the end of my desk, along with a cheerful note from Mathilde reminding me that failure to return them at the end of the day was an 'Article Twelve' offense... and wishing me a nice day.

Despite Kayce Cullen's best efforts to explain, I still didn't really understand anything that had happened since the day she'd shown up at my door with an arrest warrant. But it had been a long time since I'd really understood much of anything, and I was inclined to trust her—if not Hiram Díaz.

Once my 'net terminal was powered up and I remembered how to check my messages, I found out that I also had an appointment—and that I was already late.

I was later still by the time I made it to the office I'd been told to report to on another floor of the BSI building. The meeting notice had simply said 'Dr. Abenard,' and included a time and a room number.

The room reminded me of a doctor's office reception area, right down to the old magazines sitting on an end table next to a sofa. At a desk at the end of the room sat a small woman in civilian dress and a lab coat, with dark hair pulled back in a bun. When I entered, she was staring intently at a 'net terminal through glasses with severe black Citizen Allotment frames.

"Apologies for being late," I said. "I'm here to see Dr. Abenard."

She looked up. Through the glasses, the eyes were dark and piercing. "No apologies needed, Sr. Ellsberg. It's only your second day, and this place can be intimidating. I'm Helene Abenard. I'm neither so busy nor so important as to need a receptionist. Please come this way."

I followed her into an inner office that was lined with bookshelves. In one corner sat a chair, next to a couch. It was a familiar set up. "You're a psychist," I said.

"Correct," said Dr. Abenard. "And you are a man who has very interesting and troubling dreams. My friend Hiram thinks I can help with that. Please make yourself comfortable."

"No offense, doctor, but I've seen therapists before. A lot of them. It hasn't helped."

"Perhaps this time it will, señor."

"Other that I'm being paid to do this, what would be any different?"

"Perhaps more than you know," said Dr. Abenard. "The objectives are different in this instance, and I start out with one very different assumption from any other 'therapist' you have seen in the past." She removed her glasses. Her eyes were larger, darker, and more intense without them, seemed to grow even larger as she spoke. "You see, Sr. Ellsberg, I happen to know that your dreams are real. The way I am going to help you is by finding out why."

* * * *

On the third day, I got my collection back.

A few days after I had first been 'hired,' a cargo van had arrived at my apartment to retrieve the crates of assorted fanzines I'd promised Díaz, as well as my back catalog of unpublished manuscripts, as well as my dream journals. It had felt like signing my life away.

Now it was all back, filling the shelves across the back of my office.

I found a note sitting on top of my 'net term keyboard. It read: "Not to leave premises, of course, but use as needed for your research. Regards, HD."

Not too surprisingly, Mystery Disks Revealed was not included.

By the end of the week, I had submitted my first set of reports. The material I'd been asked to analyze included not just numerous mystery disk and ghost airship sightings, but stranger material as well. Accounts of 'mowing devils,' 'swamp apes,' even 'sea serpents.' I could truthfully say that most of it reminded me of nothing I had ever seen, conscious or dreaming.

But not all of it... and particularly not the mystery disk sightings. I began to detect a pattern. A pattern that I decided I was better off keeping to myself.

I received a follow-up message informing me that my session with Dr. Abenard was now a weekly occurrence. I knew that not going wasn't really an option, but I thought about it, anyway. I've never really liked pyschists. The fact that this one apparently didn't think I was crazy was not an incredible improvement. I could not clearly recall much about my first session at all... and that bothered me even more.

But it was still the best-paying job I'd ever had. And they really had said they'd help.

nine: kayce

"Okay, people—your next assignment is an analysis of the role played by British naval intervention in American revolutions of the 19th century. If you think Californianos have a republic because God wanted it that way, you are very much enrolled in the wrong class. I want specific examples. I want some real research. Please 'net message me if you have any questions. Class dismissed."

I had a meeting scheduled with the admiral. If I hurried,
I might have time for a latte. Shouldering my briefbag,
I made my way out of the Academy and headed across the quad to Admin Tower. Hopefully, there would not be too many people queued up at the cafe. I was passing the statue of Grand Admiral Castro when my phone

buzzed. It was a message from Mathilde, letting me know the meeting had been postponed 15 minutes. Good. I really needed that latte.

It was a nice day. The fog had burned off, the sky was blue. Across the bay, the San Francisco skyline glittered in the sun. Hopefully, this meeting would not go too long. Esmerelda and I had opera tickets, and I needed to retrieve my dress whites from the cleaners. I felt a moment of apprehension when I saw something else glittering, high in the sky, then relief when I realized it was just a rocket plane on final approach to the aerodrome.

I really hate it when that happens. It's happened a lot lately.

* * * *

There had been a queue at the cafe, but my favorite barista was on duty and had my drink waiting for me as soon as I got to the counter. I made it to the meeting with minutes to spare. At the head of the table sat Admiral Díaz, for once in standard uniform. Next to him were two men with matching buzz cuts and dark suits. Estaditos, from the looks of them, one darker and one grayer. The suits were severely tailored in typical U.S. fashion, both adorned with the 'Flag and Party' lapel pins that had become common among Estaditos since their unfortunate recent election... among other things.

Across the table from them was the psychist working with Saul Ellsberg, Dr. Abernard. I took the seat next to her. The admiral nodded to Mathilde, who withdrew and closed the door.

"Good afternoon, Commander Cullen," the admiral said. "I'm glad you could join us. These gentlemen are members of the U.S. contingent within Majestic. Colonels Hodge and Blaine, U.S. Air Force, on permanent assignment to the U.S. Defense Intelligence Agency as liaison to the

Advanced Studies Group at Patterson Aerodrome. They are operating with precisely the same level of security clearance as ourselves."

"Understood, sir." One of the first things I'd been briefed on about Majestic was what to share and what not to share. The Estaditos had tried to have it both ways more than once, were hardly any more to be trusted now than when they had tried to bomb Pearl Harbor. An agreement had been reached, decades before, to share information on alien technology in their possession they could not decipher without our help. Everything else was off the table.

"Commander Cullen is a recent addition to the Majestic group, although an analyst of some years standing within BSI. She is also an instructor at our Naval Academy. Recent findings and events have led me to believe it would be beneficial to include someone with the commander's specific expertise in our investigation. Going forward, she will be a routine attendee of these briefings.

"The purpose of this meeting," the admiral continued, "is to share our findings to date regarding Projects Oneiros and Ikelos. In turn, our colleagues from DIA will share current findings of their own." He turned to me. "Commander Cullen, this will include some information you are cleared to receive that has not been included in your previous briefings. You will have an opportunity to ask questions."

I nodded. At some point, convincing myself it was all some elaborate hoax had stopped being an option. There had been a number of curious redactions in the materials I'd been given. If even half of those redactions got filled in... this might be the most interesting meeting I had attended in a long, long time.

"Let us begin with the DIA report. Colonels?"

"Thank you, Admiral." The younger of the two, Hodge, removed a single page of notes from his briefcase, glanced over them for a moment. "When the Majestic commission was formed, one of the greatest concerns driving it was the apparent ability of unknown aircraft to enter North American airspace without detection. Over time, greater emphasis was given to pure science. But this remains, at its core, a defense alliance—we must be able to defend American airspace."

Interesting choice of words, I thought. 'American,' not 'North American.' Was he being deliberately provocative... or did he just not know any better?

"In view of the recent escalation of such incursions, DIA has prioritized this vulnerability above all other stated concerns in the Majestic mission statement. The technical details will be forthcoming, but we have been authorized to share this: we now have a high-reliability means of detecting such 'nonlocal' incursions—as they occur."

"And this has been tested?" Admiral Díaz asked. "How reliable is 'high reliability'?"

"The reliability is at least comparable to the earliest radiowave detection units," Colonel Hodge said. "We've tested it the one way we have at our disposal—by cycling the Device."

"That is very close to a violation of our agreement, Colonel. After all the decades we've invested in finding the starter switch, it should be a great pity if you damaged it."

Blaine, the older officer, responded. "We felt the risk was warranted, and I suspect your government will agree. Is this a matter we need to escalate?"

Díaz shook his head. "Not if what you say can be verified. How soon will these 'technical details' be available?"

"We have in our possession the entire data dump of cleared material on encrypted digital media. I was instructed to deliver it to you personally. You can sign for it any time you wish."

"And you believe this solution applies equally to all such 'non-local incursions'?"

Blaine turned to Hodge. "I'm letting you take that one."

The younger officer nodded. "Even though evidence suggests multiple sources for non-local incursions, we believe that of these intruders are using variations on the same technology to get here. Unfortunately, this does not rule out other possible technologies in use as well. There is evidence these technologies may include various means of concealment, affecting both radiowave detection and visual sightings."

"In other words," Díaz said, "you don't know."

Blaine responded. Despite having the same rank, it was becoming obvious which one was in charge. "We believe gravimetric variance detection should be effective for the majority of non-local incursions. The remainder, I believe, fall in your team's special area of expertise."

"Point taken," the admiral said. "And—to be clear—it is an impressive accomplishment. What to do with it is not a matter for today's agenda, in any case. I do have a question though, Colonel Blaine—if I may."

"By all means, Admiral."

"What is meant by 'cleared material'? Is the data you have brought us not complete?"

Blaine sighed. "It is as complete as it can be at this time, complete enough to verify the detection system's accuracy and reliability. I have not seen the complete data either, Admiral. Homeland Security is conducting their own analysis of certain components of the system and refuse to release that information until their analysis has been completed. My apologies, Admiral, if you find this frustrating—I feel that way myself, actually—but this comes straight from Director Stone."

"I am unsurprised," Admiral Díaz replied.

Neither was I. The U.S. Department of Federal Domestic Security, AKA 'Homeland Security' wasn't exactly the Yanqui equivalent of BSI—they're not military, we don't spy on our own citizens—but their similar role in the Majestic alliance, once minimal, had steadily escalated over the years. After the most recent U.S. elections, that escalation had increased sharply.

"Colonel, this comes even closer to a violation of the agreement—and this time, I may very well choose to escalate," the admiral continued. "Do you have any idea how long Director Stone intends to sit on your data?"

"Actually, I do," Blaine said. "The director has promised full disclosure and an opportunity for a full review at the upcoming annual joint conference."

"How very convenient," the admiral observed. "Ah well, it is what is. When next you report to him, do give the Director my regards. Commander Cullen," he turned to me. "Do you have any questions?"

I shook my head. Everything I needed to know about 'the Device' had either already been answered or was as unknown to these Estaditos as it was to me.

"No? Very well, then. I do not regard this matter as settled, but clearly, nothing further can be done today. Let us proceed then to the matter of Project Oneiros. Dr. Abenard is both a certified psychist and a licensed mesmerist who has worked with numerous individuals with experiences similar to her current subject. I would like your report next, Doctor."

"Thank you, Admiral." Helene Abenard was even shorter than I was, with enormous dark eyes behind heavy glasses. Like Saul, she was a civilian contractor for BSI with a deliberately vague contract. Like myself, she had been recruited by Admiral Díaz to carry out research of a very specific and very secret nature—that apparently now fell within my 'need to know.'

She opened a folder and read from her notes. "I have had several sessions to date with 'Patient Alpha' under varying levels of mesmeric induction. He has no conscious memories of abduction experience, nor can any such memories be uncovered, even at very deep levels of mesmerization. It appears that he is very much telling the truth when he states that he has received sensitive information via dreams."

"Is there a particular reason," Colonel Hodge asked, "why this 'Patient Alpha' is not being identified by name?"

"Many," replied Admiral Díaz, "Beginning with the fact that he is a Citizen of the Republic of California with certain guaranteed rights... including that of privacy."

"Excuse me," I said. "Abduction?"

"We'll get to that," the admiral said. "Just not yet. Doctor, please continue."

Dr. Abenard nodded. "The details of confidential information this individual should not possess are striking. However, other details have emerged that are simply... puzzling."

"Puzzling in what way, Doctor?" asked Colonel Hodge.

"Puzzling in that they neither conform to what the patient states when not mesmerized or events as we know them. For example, under deep mesmeric induction the subject insists that the crash the Device was recovered from did not occur in Corona, Texas, but in someplace called 'Roswell, New Mexico.'"

"I'm sorry, New Mexico?" asked the other colonel. Blaine, I reminded myself.

"I know," said Dr. Abenard. "It makes no sense. I even asked him where this 'New Mexico' was. He told me it was in the United States."

The colonels looked at each other. "News to us," one of them said.

Part 5: Collegium Invisibilia

one: murphy

Basically, I had just seen my first 'UFO.'

The fact that I'd hitched numerous rides in The Order's flying saucers over the years and had once led an assault team of Reptilians under fire from a Grey mothership didn't count—I knew what those things were.

This was truly 'unidentified.'

"Ghost airship?" I said to no one in particular.

"For all I know," answered the no one in particular who lived in my head. "You're the expert on this stuff, not me."

In my own world, a century of hot and cold running warfare had spurred technology that had never happened here. In this world, airships of the non-ghost variety were fairly common, as were autogyros. The highest of aviation high tech were suborbital rocket planes and extreme high-altitude aerostats. Anything like what I'd just seen? Not even close.

I turned and looked at Case's data ghost avatar. "Would you know Grey tech if you saw it?"

"I think so," he said. "And I don't think that was one of theirs. What about your buddies?"

"I can only speak to what I've seen—and that's a new one on me as well. We can talk tomorrow, Case. I'm still human, more or less. I need sleep."

"Just don't leave 'social interface' switched off for a week, OK?"

"No worries, there's too much going on. We'll talk in the morning."

* * * *

I'd slept long and hard. For once, I had been untroubled by dreams. As soon as I'd swilled down some cowboy coffee, it was time to check in with Case.

"Good morning," he said as he flickered into existence.

"How would you know?"

"That it's morning? I can access the clock chip in your implants. I don't know if it's 'good' or not. You tell me."

"When I figure it out, you'll be the first to know. Meanwhile, I'm hoping there are a few other things you can tell me about... starting with my implants and the instincts that got me out of a jam twenty miles up that road."

"You want to know what they did to you."

"Anything you actually know about that... yeah, that would be nice."

"I don't know anything more about the physical stuff than you do—less, really. But the whole reason I'm even here is that there was an open channel into your brain the entire time you were in cold sleep. They pumped a lot of stuff into you. Between the rejuvenation therapy and a new set of conditioned reflexes, you've been ramped up to a new level of badass, old buddy. If someone puts a live round in your head, you're still dead. But anyone who gets close enough to try to grab your sidearm is probably going to wind up about like 'Sheriff Johnson.'"

"That much is reassuring. Anything else get uploaded besides you and some new fighting skills?"

"I'm not sure what you mean."

186

"What I mean is that my dedication to completing this mission is beginning to disturb me. Any possibility it isn't really mine?"

"Funny you should ask. That's a question I can answer."

"Please do," I said.

The data ghost/avatar of my old friend 'walked' to the edge of the ruin I'd spent the night in and looked out into the gathering morning light. "I've known you a long time, Murphy. I've seen you keep faith with drug dealers that would've cut out your liver for a spare peso, saw you move heaven and earth and back yourself into a corner over a marriage you couldn't possibly save.

"I saw you keep your word to me, time after time after time—long after you had other allegiances and no real reason to give a shit about me or the people I answered to.

"You aren't being manipulated, you aren't being controlled. You may've been rebuilt from the DNA out... but the essentials are still the same. Does it make any sense that you're determined to keep your word to the 'people' who sent you here? Not even slightly. Is it who you fundamentally are?

"Pretty much, old buddy... pretty much."

two: kayce

"Why do you keep looking at the sky?"

"I didn't know I was. I'm sorry."

"You do that a lot lately," Esmerelda said. "It is a little disturbing, Corazon."

"Please think nothing of it." It was a nice evening; we splurged and hired a carriage for the opera. I should be paying attention to my wife, not the night sky.

Sometimes opposites really do attract. Esmerelda is willowy and tall in ways that I am short and compact, as dark as I am fair. I am a blunt pragmatist who teaches history from the perspective of gunboat diplomacy. She collects, curates, and creates art. Why a gifted and creative woman from an old Californiano family had fallen in love with a butch little gringa academic was an even more profound mystery to me than all of the ghost airships and mystery disks of the world wrapped up into one big glob of impossibility. But unlike the other mystery, this was one that made me very happy.

"I will 'think nothing' when you stop doing it," she said. "The carriage was a lovely idea. You should enjoy it."

"Oh, I do, Corazon—very much. We should have more champagne, I think."

She smiled. "I agree."

* * * *

The Majestic briefing had raised as many questions as it answered—at least for me.

The thing that had fallen from the sky in 1947 was no more 'technology' in any sense we could clearly understand than what seemed to be its crew was in any sense human. But after half a century of study, we at least had some idea of what it was and what it did—even if how it actually worked remained as impenetrable as ever.

Deciphering the remains of the crew had been relatively simple by comparison.

"It still makes no sense that they should look even slightly like us," the admiral had said. "But at least we now know why." Dr. Abenard had finished her report and answered every question I'd had—including a few I was beginning to regret having ever asked. It would shortly be my turn.

"We had independently reached similar conclusions," said Colonel Blaine. "Although we're as much at a loss when it comes to a point of origin as you are. The one conclusion from available data doesn't make any sense."

"Which does not make it untrue," said Admiral Díaz. "An advanced study group at the Pacific Institute of Technology has recently proposed a new model for the deep structure of physical reality. That model provides for quite a few possible 'points of origin.'"

"I've seen the paper in question," Blaine replied. "No offense to your old alma mater, but it sounds like another PacTech prank to me."

"No offense taken," said the admiral, "Although at this point, interdimensional wormholes make as much sense as anything else I've heard proposed. Not a matter for today's agenda, in any case. Commander Cullen," He turned to me. "I believe it is your turn. Please proceed."

"Thank you, Admiral." After Dr. Abenard's report, mine was going to be a distinct anticlimax.

"My role in this project has been, so far, a logical extension of my academic career and previous role within BSI. Typically, I am given field reports and asked to analyze them. In this case, worldwide reports of unexplained phenomena dating back to roughly 5,000 BCE."

"Excuse me," said the other colonel, Hodge. "And no offense, Commander Cullen—but I am unsure I see any relevance to this. The Majestic partnership has a specific scope. It does not include historic research... or the rest of the world."

"Permit me, Commander," Díaz said, then turned to Hodge. "I disagree. Majestic was formed to assess a threat. We need to know the scope of that threat. We now have clear evidence the threat has been in place for at least a century longer than previously supposed. What if it goes further back than that? There could be other artifacts to examine; there could be other artifacts that are being examined. We've no evidence of any other groups like 'Majestic' outside of North America—but what if that merely means our counterparts in Europe and Asia are better at hiding such things than ourselves? 'Mystery Disks' piloted by the German Luftwaffe would certainly be no less a threat than any such craft arriving from other worlds."

But possibly just as much threat, I thought, as mystery disks piloted by the likes of Colonel Hodge—particularly if his view of 'the rest of the world' came anywhere
close to his current commander in chief.

The senior colonel, Blaine, stepped in. "None of this is anything new, Colonel Hodge, and Admiral Díaz is right. The scope of the Majestic alliance has been debated for years. The California contingent has always had a broader perspective. Let's hear Commander Cullen's report."

I continued. "You're correct, Colonel: It's not a new concept. Some years ago, a book entitled Ancient Aethernauts proposed that much of human history was a direct result of intervention by creatures not of this world. Don't be surprised if you've never heard of it—it's not a particularly good book.

"My own analysis comes to somewhat different conclusions," I continued. "I found significant evidence of aerial phenomena corresponding to 'ghost airships' and 'mystery disks' going back many thousands of years—only to stop abruptly at the beginning of the modern era, then resume again in the late nineteenth century."

"Define 'modern era,'" Blaine said.

"Late fifteenth to early seventeenth century... say 1600 or so. 'Patient Zero' has been asked to review the same material under my direction, given deliberately vague criteria on what he was looking for. I have not seen his reports."

"That would be my doing," Admiral Díaz said. "Consider it a double-blind study of sorts. My own report will be forthcoming to the Majestic senior planning group—also at the next joint conference."

"I look forward to it," Blaine said. "Meanwhile, I'd like to hear Commander Cullen's conclusions."

* * * *

"You are doing it again."

The opera had been nice, even though I doubt I ever would've acquired a taste for it were it not for Esmerelda's civilizing influence. But I enjoyed putting on dress whites and 'doing the town.' Why live in one of the greatest cities on Earth if you don't get out once in a while and actually enjoy it?

It had gotten quite a bit cooler by the time the carriage we'd hired called at the opera house to take us home. Esmerelda was curled up next to me under both a carriage blanket and the largely ornamental wrap she had worn to match her dress. I had stuffed a scarf down the front of my service overcoat. A fresh bottle of champagne had replaced the one we'd emptied earlier.

And yes. I was staring at the sky.

"You tell me that the work you do for Hiram Díaz is boring, and I believe you—for Hiram is boring. He is vain and self-absorbed, and whatever service he is doing the republic, you may be sure it is as much service to himself. My mother almost married him, you know. I know your admiral fairly well."

"You've mentioned it before." Basically, every time we ever talk about my job.

"Well, this is different, corazon. Whatever Hiram has dragged you into this time is terrifying you, and that terrifies me—for you are fearless, my darling. I am your wife. Whatever secrets you share with me, I will take to my grave... you know this."

"I do know that."

"Then tell me what this is. What is it you expect to see when you look into the skies?"

three: ellsberg

For weeks, the material I was being asked to analyze had been getting stranger and stranger. If I was still writing fiction for a living, I could've easily sold a story or two out of it. There were also things I recognized from my dreams, which were also becoming stranger, increasingly vivid and more than occasionally prophetic.

But for the first time in my life, I wasn't frightened by them.

This might've been thanks to the sessions with Dr. Abenard. I still found her unsettling, was not at all crazy about being 'mesmerized.' But whatever she was doing while I was in a trance state I could not remember seemed to be helping me.

At Kayce's suggestion, I'd even joined a gym for the first time in my life.

"You'd look better, Saul. You'd also feel better. Anyhow, it's part of the benefits package you get as a defense contractor—so why not?"

Even when she didn't have a few hundred kilos of Shore Patrol as backup, it was pretty much impossible to argue with Kayce Cullen… for the most part, I didn't even try.

At some point, I had simply stopped thinking about the utter unlikelihood of it all… and just went with it. I still resented the high-handed way Hiram Díaz had 'recruited' me, but I had to admit, he might've saved my life.

I still had a hard time believing that Navy Intelligence was willing to pay me to review 'ghost airship' reports, but I was consistently paying my rent on time for the first time in my adult life. I still lived in the same third-floor walkup in The Mission, and I still dreamed about impossible things that occasionally came true—the worst of which still haunts me, whether I'm asleep or awake. But almost everything else had changed.

Kayce Cullen had become something of a friend, or at least seemed to be, to the point where I actually felt bad about the way I'd ogled her backside while she was arresting me. After I'd been on the job for a few weeks, she'd invited me to meet her for coffee at the RCN Admin Tower again. "I have something for you," she said.

"This time, I'm buying," I told her.

Sitting in her preferred spot with a view of the bay, she reached into her briefbag, handed me a parcel wrapped in brown paper. Handing her the latte she'd ordered, I opened it.

"Nice," I said, "but I already have a couple of copies."

"Not like this. Take a look inside,"

It was a hardbound copy of Scourge of the Aether Patrol. The inscription on the flyleaf read, "Best regards, Saul—if you're ever up for hitting the Fresno Con again, let me know."

"I'm amazed he really remembered me—thanks. This isn't going to get either of us in trouble, is it?"

"Pops remembers everyone, Saul," she told me. "I just told him you were on a writing assignment for BSI. He knows I can't really talk about my work—and no, it won't get you in trouble."

Meanwhile, the mystery disk reports kept coming in at ever-increasing rates. Sometimes, the reports that hit my desk had notes attached in Díaz's handwriting, which was as sloppy and oversized as Díaz himself. Not infrequently, I'd see the same reports in the newspapers, with oddly inconsistent details.

Díaz had been true to his word that I'd be well treated. Whether or not I would ever have any 'answers' to any of it didn't seem any more likely than anyone ever thinking that what I was doing was in any way 'important.'

I'd fallen into a routine that was strangely comforting and utterly unlike my previous life as a freelance writer. The one connection to my past: I still got fan mail.

I still had the same mailbox I'd had for years. I liked to hear from people who liked my work, just not enough to publish my home address. As it happens, the post office was a block from my train stop, so it was easy enough to check my mail on the way to or from my new job. Most of what showed up in the box was trash these days.

But not all of it.

I'd had a funny feeling when I saw the manila envelope with a Republic of Texas return address—call it déjà vu. When I opened the envelope, the feeling got even stronger. I was on my way to work. I caught the train and read what I'd received. By the time I arrived at the Naval Preserve transit station, I wasn't happy... but I knew what I had to do.

four kayce

"If you think this funny, corazon, you will notice I am not laughing."

Of course she had not believed me. I hadn't really expected she would. But secrets destroy marriages, and the toll taken by BSI is legendary. It was not going to happen to us, if I could help it. In an open carriage riding home from an opera, I made a decision. Apparently, not a good one.

"I'm not either. I wish I was." We were sitting in the living room of our townhouse. To offset the chill of the ride home, I'd started a fire in the fireplace. I also poured us both brandy.

"You must think me a fool," Esmerelda seethed. "Is this nonsense Hiram's idea? If it is, he will pay."

"If you say anything of any of this to Hiram Díaz, I'll be the one who pays." I poured more brandy. Esmerelda's went down in an instant. I decided not to pour any more. "If you say anything to anyone... I will pay."

My wife had wanted to know why I kept looking at the sky. Against Navy regulations (and better sense), I'd told her. I never should've joined The Bureau. I'm just not good enough at lying.

"This is like the nonsense your father writes." She was still angry, but seemed to be calming down. I'd been through it before. As long as I didn't get mad as well, everything would turn out okay.

Maybe.

"That's what I thought, too," I told her. "Unfortunately, it happens to be real."

"Little green people from Mars?"

"Grey, actually... and we don't really know where they are from."

"And they are here... why?"

"We don't know that, either. But I think we're about to find out."

* * * *

"You've done great this semester, everyone—now we get to deal with the fun stuff. For your final, I need a detailed analysis of the events leading up to the Treaty of Vera Cruz, including the failed attack on Pearl Harbor and the formation of the Pacific and Northwest Federation.

"We all know the world did not go to war—I need to know that you know why it didn't... or at least that you're able to make a convincing guess. Give it some thought, people. Anyone who can't show up next week prepared to write at least two thousand words on the subject is not getting a passing grade. Class dismissed; have a great weekend."

For once, there were no staff meetings or emergencies or conferences with snotty yanqui colonels. If I hurried, I could be home in time to freshen up for Esmerelda's opening, maybe even get some dinner first.

Of course, my phone buzzed as soon as I left the Academy. Fate was determined to wreck my marriage. I should probably just get used to the idea.

When I arrived at Díaz's office, Mathilde favored me with a sympathetic look as she buzzed me in. I knew that she knew that the job was making my home life hell. She knew that I knew that there wasn't a damned thing any of us could do about it.

I immediately noticed the warning signs as I walked in.

The admiral's desk was spotlessly clean, with the exception of two Navy file jackets, both labeled 'Above Top Secret.' Except for the lack of a tie, the admiral was more or less in standard uniform. Something was going on.

He returned my salute and waved me into a guest chair that was conspicuously clear of unfiled state secrets. "Apologies, Commander," he said. "I know your wife is unveiling some new art this evening; I will do my best to not keep you long. But there are things you need to see." Warning sign number three. When I stop being 'Kayce' and start being 'Commander,' things have gotten serious.

As I took the proffered seat, the admiral opened one of the file jackets and drew out a crudely reproduced and bound 'magazine,' entitled Aethernauts Among Us? which had been sealed in clear cellophane to which a label had been affixed which read 'CLEAN ROOM ONLY.'

"This looks unfortunately familiar," I said.

"As well it should. The typography and, apparent bindery and printing stock are an exact match to Mystery Disks Revealed. It even claims the same nonexistent address in Texas for the publisher. Your research assistant has some interesting fans—regardless of his lack of recent published work."

"Saul?"

"Sr. Ellsberg keeps a mailbox in Pioneer Square, which he apparently checks as part of his commute to this office. Upon his arrival yesterday, he gave this to Mathilde."

"More Texas Air Corps press releases?"

"Not quite, although it does reproduce a fairly entertaining story from something called 'The Huitlacoche Herald,' regarding an unfortunate encounter between a local law enforcement officer and what the author of this publication insists on describing as an 'undercover aethernaut.'"

I've hated that word ever since Pops came up with it. 'Ancient Aethernauts' had been bad enough. Now, apparently, they came in an undercover variety as well. "I assume there's more, sir."

"Very much more, Commander. Once Mathilde brought this to my attention, I sent both this publication and our copy of Mystery Disks Revealed to the materials analysis lab for a detailed comparison. I wanted to determine if they were, indeed, from the same source."

"I take it you have the results?"

"Not quite the results I expected, but yes. The lab confirmed that these publications were produced in precisely the same manner, most probably using the same equipment. Having a second artifact provided an opportunity for an even more detailed analysis. The results are somewhat... unsettling.

"This is not paper, however much it resembles it to the touch. The images and words were not printed, photocopied, painted, or placed by any other process we know. They are an integral part of whatever this stuff is. Even the bindery, which resembles the work of a cheap office stapler, is not what it seems. Only the envelope this was mailed in could be identified as something manufactured by any known process."

"What does this mean, sir?"

"It means a number of things. It means your 'need to know' just escalated—and so has Sr. Ellsberg's. I told you once that he was not what he seemed. It is time now to tell you just what that means." He handed me the other file jacket. Below the secrecy classification was another label... which simply read 'Project Oneiros'—the project for which Helene Abenard and Saul Ellsberg had both been hired.

"I'm already cleared for this, Admiral."

"Not all of it—not until now. This will explain much," Díaz said. "It may not leave this office."

five: murphy

It had been one of those pivotal elections that change everything. On the one hand, a member of an American political dynasty with an unfortunate sense of entitlement and a shitton of baggage. On the other hand, a crass outsider with a weakness for conspiracy theories and a low talent for exploiting the racist tendencies of their political 'base.'

Against the expectations of the media and the political establishment, the vulgar racebaiter won the election and changed history—at least in our world.

In the universe I now inhabited, Andrew Jackson never had a chance.

After I got out of the badlands, more research into the 'second objective' of my mission seemed like a good idea. Even though the public libraries in Texas weren't as good as they were in Oregon, they were good enough. There were some possible added benefits to the particular library I was sitting in, depending on how much the librarian cared about local and regional esoterica. Gradual improvements in highway signage and paving as I made my way south meant that I had fully crossed through the badlands and into the Republic of Texas.

At a rest stop, I had shaved and returned my sidearm to my bag of tricks. If I made my way into the more civilized parts of Texas looking like an outlaw biker, it seemed not unlikely that I might wind up being treated like one. Comparing the jails in this version of 'Texas' with the ones I remembered from my misspent youth was a bit of crosstime comparative analysis I preferred to pass on to some other researcher.

In order for it to be a fair comparison, though, I would've had to have gotten busted in New Mexico as well as Texas in my younger days—since on the other side of the wormhole, that's where I'd be right now.

"We're being watched, dude."

I was leaving the 'social interface' switched on a lot more lately. If I wanted his opinion on the stuff I was reading/ recording, it was easier if Case had already 'seen' it. And his point about seeing things I didn't notice had been underscored by having a close encounter of the second kind in the high desert, as well as a crooked cop almost getting the drop on me.

"Watched by who?" I muttered. In order for Case to hear me, I actually had to speak. It didn't have to be my normal speaking voice, though—just loud enough to hear myself, which meant he could pick it up from my implants.

"The librarian. She's been glancing this way for most of the last half hour. Maybe she thinks you're hot."

"Or not." I could almost make out the librarian's desk from the corner of my eye. Case, having full access to my peripheral vision, could evidently see it perfectly. "What do you recommend?"

"I recommend that you straighten up in your chair and say 'hi' to the nice lady—she's headed this way."

"Discúlpeme, señor, ¿habla inglés?" said a female voice behind me.

"I do," I said as I turned. "¿Qué prefieres, señora?"

"English, I think," she replied. The librarian who Case claimed had been watching me was a woman of average height and build, perhaps as young as late thirties, as old as mid-forties, with olive complexion, solemn gray eyes, aquiline features, and a thick mane of dark, curly hair.

She was wearing a longsleeved gray dress that matched her eyes, and a dark cardigan and dark hose to match her hair. 'Pythia Cortes' read the name tag pinned to her cardigan. "The library will be closing quite soon," she told me. "And you have taken from the shelves quite a number of books that you obviously are not really reading, that I shall have to reshelve. I'm going to have to work late as it stands; I'd rather not have to work any later."

"I certainly don't want to make you work late," I said, "but I really am reading these books."

"I'm sorry, sir, but you are just flipping pages—no one reads that fast."

"I do, and I'll prove it." I handed her the opened book I'd been reading, subvocally muttered, "Stick the last page I looked at on heads-up."

Case chuckled in my head. "God, but you're a dick. Here you go, old buddy."

The page materialized before my eyes, and I started reading it aloud. After a couple of paragraphs, she cut me off.

"Impressive," she said, "and I apologize. But I still have to reshelve all these books."

"I'll make you a deal," I said. "I'll reshelve every single book I have read, put it exactly where I found it. You'll get off from work on time, maybe even early. And then I will buy you a drink."

She smiled a small, grave smile. "I do not drink, but I often have coffee after I am done here. Help me close the library, and you are very welcome to join me."

* * * *

In the aftermath of a failed rebellion by entitled sons of bitches that thought they had a right to own other sons of bitches, Texas had wound up a buffer state between the U.S. and California... as well as a convenient dumping ground for former slave owners who'd managed to escape hanging.

Three-term president John Quincy Adams was far more interested in crushing slave power in the Southern U.S. than pursuing western expansion. The end result was a 'United States' that pretty much ended at the Mississippi River, a Republic of Texas running up the middle of the continent, and a Pacific federation that included Oregon, California, the

Kingdom of Hawai'i, most of what I was used to thinking of as British Columbia, and the Alaska Panhandle. It still took almost as long to fully expunge slavery from all of North America as it had in my world—the institution lingered in the southern end of Texas for almost a generation, with consequences that never really went away.

Even though it ended at the Mississippi River, the United States had been dominant in North America up until the closing decades of the 19th century, when a resource-rich and technologically advanced California pulled ahead... and stayed there.

Now that I was back in Texas, I was no longer calling myself a 'Texican.' I was now the probable anomaly of a half-Centroamericano / half-Californiano from Oregon Territory, making his way south to visit long-estranged relatives. It wasn't perfect—this version of Texas was even more profoundly racist than the one I grew up in, despite an even larger Hispanic population. But it was probable... and that's usually good enough.

And at least here, my manufactured Californiano pesos were just as good as my manufactured U.S. dollars. A good thing—I was running short on both.

As I had crossed the midcontinent desert and headed south, the sense of going back in time only grew greater. This was a 'Texas' far more reminiscent of old movies than the one I remembered from my childhood.

It was a place where my dad could've gone as he pleased, my mamacita would've wanted to stick close to my dad, and I would've gotten beaten up routinely by just about everyone on general principles. I wasn't too worried about getting beaten up, even though the rejuvenation treatment had left me looking less 'white' than ever. It had also left me with enhanced reflexes, speed, strength, and stamina. Anyone who thought I was seated at the wrong end of the lunch counter was going to have an interestingly brief time explaining the concept.

* * * *

Finishing my book, reshelving it, and reshelving the rest of what I'd read took mere minutes. I was waiting in front of the library when she walked out and locked the door behind her. It was early evening, the warmth of day beginning to give way to the cool of a desert night. I could see several shops and restaurants scattered around the plaza that might be a good place to obtain a coffee. If Pythia Cortes had anything else in mind, the Armstrong was parked nearby.

I'd taken advantage of the time waiting for her to have a brief conversation with Case. He had manifested his avatar as soon as I'd left the library, dressed in what he apparently thought was location-appropriate wardrobe. "Dude," I told him. "It's a good thing no one can see you but me. No one here dresses like that."

"No one here dresses like you either, old buddy. You planning on starting a 'Clash' revival band?"

"Nope, and I kinda doubt there's much market here for 'The Village People' either—but if I hear anything, I'll let you know. Meanwhile—and no offense—I'm switching 'social' off for a bit."

"Aw, you're no fun."

"It's just coffee, Case—but I'd still like a little privacy."

The ghost in my head chuckled as he faded from view. "Yeah, right. Just don't do anything I wouldn't do."

The preferred destination for coffee turned out to be a little panadería across the plaza from the library—which was just as well: I had a hard time imagining Pythia Cortes in the Armstrong's sidecar, much less doing anything as undignified as straddling the bike behind me. She had added a gray beret to her outfit by the time she'd joined me. I found myself wishing I had taken the time to improve upon my own wardrobe.

"Thank you for joining me," I said, as we strolled across the plaza. "I apologize again if my research caused any undue work for you."

The invitation for a drink had been a sudden impulse. The only human interaction I'd had in this world since I'd left Oregon Territory had involved incapacitating a larcenous small-town sheriff. Whatever Case might think, my intentions were—at least as far as I knew—entirely honorable.

"Thank you for offering, Mister...?"

"Murphy. No need for the 'mister.'"

"Just 'Murphy'? I find that awkward. What is your full name?"

"My full name is Miguel Estefan Alejandro Murphy... but I have not used it in a long time."

"I shall call you Miguel," she said firmly. "It is a nice name—I cannot imagine why you do not use it."

The panadería had a small number of outside tables, we took one and ordered. The coffee turned out to have been brewed with cinnamon and arrived topped with heavy cream dusted with nutmeg. On impulse, I ordered as well a small serving of savory shortbreads that reminded me of things my mamacita had once enjoyed baking. The sky was cloudless, deepening toward indigo as the sun slipped below the nearby hills.

I sipped my coffee and reminisced. It had been a long time since anyone had called me 'Miguel.'

"'Pythia' is a nice name as well, but not very common. I was named for my uncles. Who were you named for?"

"No one in particular. My mother's family is Greek; the name has meaning there."

"Particularly in Delphi," I said.

She smiled. "When I first saw you, I thought you were just some transient pretending to read books. You are not what you seem, Miguel."

"I'm just a man on a mission—but I'm glad I seemed someone you'd like to have coffee with."

"I admit to being intrigued. I have read of people who could read a page at a glance and remember what they had read, but I had not expected I would ever meet one. Have you always had such abilities?"

"You could pretty much say that's how I came into this world."

* * * *

The priorities of the 'mission' I'd accepted from the Obligate were changing.

In terms of my primary objective, delivering pseudo-Dawn Matter devices to a possible archangel in Central America, the main change was timing. After my close encounter in the high desert, it was obvious this universe was not quite so isolated from the multiverse at large as the Obligate believed. Something was here, apparently had been for some time.

From my years in the Order, I had a better than average knowledge of what most people would call 'aliens.' What I had seen was something new to me. If Case was to be believed, it was new to him as well, despite his own background with aliens of a different sort.

Whether or not this 'something' had anything to do with the Selenites or shared their interest in Dawn Matter remained to be seen. But the Fortuned believed that Dawn Matter and beings made of such matter constituted a threat to all Earths across the Multiverse... should the Selenites obtain it.

They were sufficiently fearful of such a thing that they had been willing to mutate and mutilate the original Colvin Case into a thing in a tank that despaired so deeply of its own existence, it had copied itself into my implants to escape. I could all too easily imagine the Selenites, the Greys, doing something similar to the being I had befriended under the name 'Lucifer Morningstar' or whatever version of him existed in this world— although they would require a bigger tank, not to mention some serious restraints.

Then there was the secondary objective. No one had really told me why it was critical to determine this timeline's divergence from my own... but I had my own guesses.

Since slightly before humans in my timeline stopped hanging out in trees, The Fortuned had operated as the epitome of 'exceptionalism' across a dozen linked universes—a self-appointed chosen people locked in existential combat against a collectivist alien other, with the Obligate as the frontline soldiers in that endless war.

Case was right: change the scale and scope, and the rhetoric was hardly any different from the bullshit Ollie North and Poppy Bush has used to justify a half-dozen dirty little proxy wars I'd fought in and sold drugs to pay for in a younger, more brutal incarnation.

Had I signed up for yet another proxy war on behalf of yet another empire by yet another name? Maybe. But I'd been given a new life in the bargain, and I'd given my word—and even if I'd once again given it to a pack of lying, arrogant, and (this time, literally) inhuman bastards... it was still mine. I'd said I'd go 'hunting angels,' that's exactly what I was going to do.

But by the time I found any, I needed to know one hell of a lot more before I decided what to do next. And there wasn't a single library on this entire planet that could help. For all that, I'd just met a pretty nice librarian.

* * * *

"A date, eh? This time, do I get to tag along?"

"It's not exactly a date—but three's still a crowd." I was in the room I'd rented in 'downtown' Albuquerque, which in this world was scarcely more than the sleepy mission village it had started out as in mine.

"She's a girl and you're taking her out. How is it not a date?" The annoying data ghost in my head was getting more annoying than usual. I was beginning to have profound sympathy for people who hear voices that aren't really there. At least mine had an 'off' switch.

"For starters," I told him, "she thinks I'm too young for her."

It had started with an impulse to ask her to join me for a drink. One impulse leads to another, even when the drink wound up merely being coffee. After the pandería closed, we migrated to an adjacent taquería for a shared light dinner of calabacita and posole. I entertained her with a few carefully edited stories that almost explained why I was here. She told me stories, perhaps just as edited, of the life she had led in this place.

I did not expect to be invited up when I walked her to her apartment—and I wasn't. But I received a peck on the cheek as I bade her goodnight that was rewarding enough.

"Talking to you is interesting, Miguel," she'd said when we arrived at her door. Her smile had become less shy and sad as the evening progressed, but she remained grave and reserved in a way I found strangely charming.

"I'm glad you think so."

"If your research returns you to the library tomorrow, perhaps we may talk more. There is a festival in the plaza tomorrow evening, you know— perhaps I could show it to you?"

"Sure." I hadn't known, although it explained the workers I had seen hanging lanterns in trees.

The smile grew warmer. "That should be lovely. Just please don't read all the books in the library, precocious boy, and make me stay late shelving them."

"No promises, but if I do, I will again help you shelve them." For that I received another smile and demure kiss, then wandered off in the dark for my lodgings. It was all impulse on my part; what it was on her part, I couldn't say. I'd be gone soon enough, and she knew it.

I left 'social' switched off until I got back to the room, preferring the solitude of my own thoughts. I had promised to share some information with Case however, and now was as good a time as any.

* * * *

"That's it?" Case said.

I was back in my rented room, having emptied my rucksack onto the bed and shoved to one side everything that was not the Obligate field gear Case had been insisting I show him.

On the bed: a narrow black metal box, a larger box constructed from the same metal, a heavy caliber service revolver in a holster attached to a gun belt. On the other side of the bed, the data ghost's avatar looked down at my gear.

"That's all I need," I replied. "That," I pointed to the narrow box, "contains the three pseudo-Dawn Matter devices that apparently make you nervous."

"I'm pretty far past being nervous about anything, old buddy—I'm just not as trusting as you are."

"Whatever," I said. "For what it's worth, your concerns are under advisement. This," I pointed to the larger box, "is a fabricator."

"The thing you've been using to make fake money?"

"Correct. Think of it as a 3D scanner/printer. It already had some patterns loaded when I got it, and I have the option of scanning in other items as well."

"Can it print anything bigger than money?"

"Within reason," I told him. "This," I picked up the sidearm, "I believe you are reasonably familiar with."

"You mean by way of having been shot with a 'fake Glock' version of the same thing?" Case grimaced. "Yeah, somewhat. How does it work?"

"It makes a bang and blows holes in things—just like the real thing, only no ammo required. But it also has a 'nonlethal' setting, and a power supply that should last for years."

"Not to mention a trick holster," Case said. "How does that work?"

"I don't have the slightest idea," I told him. "I just know that anyone besides me who tries to unholster that hogleg is shit out of luck, and anyone who tries to fire it besides me is wasting their time. Same thing with the rucksack they gave me."

"How so?"

"Again, I don't know how it works. I just know what it does. But when I close that bag, it stays closed. When I sit it down somewhere, that somewhere is where it stays."

"I had wondered about that," Case said. "Seemed like an awfully big assumption that you weren't going to get mugged and get your toys taken away."

"It's harder than it looks," I told him.

six: ellsberg

I'd been looking at the same report for almost an hour when the phone buzzed. This particular report was something about a legendary secret society in Central America... and a pyramid that somehow seemed should be something I knew about. But if I knew anything about my dreams, I knew better than to try to force them.
Their source, whatever it was, had its own agenda.

It had been two days since Aethernauts Among Us? had turned up in my mailbox. Mathilde's face had been carefully neutral when I gave it to her. Maybe a little too neutral.

I'd had time on the train to flip through it. It was just as badly put together as its predecessor, full of the same conspiracy theory and wild speculation. The main difference was that, as far as I could tell, nothing in this pub matched up with anything I had ever dreamed—not that I was entirely sure I'd know an 'undercover Aethernaut' if I saw one, in either waking reality or dreams. The newspaper clippings used as proof of these aethernauts didn't prove much. Mostly that you could get almost anything printed as news in the Republic of Texas—and I already knew that.

At least if Admiral Díaz thought it deserved more investigation, he wouldn't have to send Kayce Cullen to arrest me again. Not that I'd complain too much if he did.

So yeah... I had sort of expected the call. "Ellsberg here."

"Hola, Saul—it's Mathilde. If you have a few minutes, the admiral would like to speak to you." Her voice was just as atypically neutral as her face had been when I'd given her the envelope two days ago. The uneasy feeling in my gut got worse, but there was really only one thing I could do about it.

"Sure," I said. "Give me a moment to get everything filed; I'll be right there."

Admiral Hiram Díaz was almost as unknown to me as the first and—so far—only time I'd met him. Kayce reported to him, I reported to Kayce. I received occasional notes and 'net messages from him, but that was it... which was fine by me.

Efforts at finding out more about him on my own hadn't gone very far. He came from an influential family, had an interesting academic career before joining the Navy. For someone who supposedly 'didn't like technology,' he'd helped the Navy develop a lot of it, mostly aerospace and electronics. He'd had a lot to do with the advances that made the 'net terminal on my desk the equal to machines that had once taken up warehouses.

After which, he had essentially dropped out of sight.

According to Who's Who, he was a member of the Admiralty Intelligence Oversight Committee and supposedly on special administrative assignment. There might have been more to be found on the Navy's private network, but I was reluctant to go looking. Accidentally getting into the wrong database was one of the things that could trade out my tiny office for an even tinier jail cell. Unlike the stuff in my dreams, Hiram Díaz was a mystery I was completely happy to leave alone.

Too bad the feeling wasn't mutual.

* * * *

Mathilde had the same carefully blank expression when she buzzed me in that she'd had the last time I'd seen her. The feeling in my gut got worse.

Díaz's office was not what I expected. Not much bigger than mine, stacked with unfiled documents I could go to jail just for knowing about—which might be about to happen, anyway.

In contrast to Mathilde's guarded expression, Díaz smiled warmly as I entered. "Hola, Sr. Ellsberg. Permit me to offer you a seat." Crossing from behind his desk, he cleared some of the top-secret clutter from the nearer of two guest chairs and shook my hand. The smile meant nothing to my gut. He'd been smiling the last time as well.

"Thank you," I said, taking the offered chair.

Díaz returned behind the desk to his own seat. "Please do not look so apprehensive," he said. "For all that we did not meet well, you have kept your end of our agreement—perhaps better than you know. I have done what I can to keep my end as well. The time has come, señor, for us both to do more.

"When you joined my team, I told you there might be a day when you were given greater access to the secrets we guard. That day has arrived. I still cannot share everything, but circumstances have increased your 'need to know'—as well as my need for your help."

* * * *

"Another round?"

"One more and done, Harry. I should head home soon."

I hadn't been in Harry's more than once or twice since I'd taken the job with BSI. At first, I'd been worried about saying something dumb and winding up with another set of armed marines at my door. Later, I found better uses for my free time—and had less of it, anyway. But this was a special occasion.

This time, I'd gotten to take the contract home with me. I could even talk to a lawyer, assuming I could find one with a security clearance. I could even go back to my old life, if I wanted to. It would be interesting, figuring out what was and was not covered by the confidentiality agreement I'd signed with BSI. I would probably have to give up Sci-Rom altogether.

Or I could sign the new contract, which would also mean giving a few things up... as well as a few things in return.

"Take the rest of the day off," the admiral had told me. "I know this is much to take in."

He was right. I'd taken the next train back into town, then realized going home was the last thing I wanted to do. Luckily, it was an easy walk from the train stop to Harry's.

This is how it works when you have dreams that come true: suddenly something you're doing or experiencing seems familiar, sometimes to the point of even knowing what someone is going to say before they say it. Then you try to remember why. Then you remember that you dreamed it.

This is how it works when you dream of impossible things: you see and experience things that do not exist in the waking world. While you are experiencing them, they are as 'real' as anything else you have ever known. In the dream, you are often yourself—but just as often someone or something very, very different. Then you wake up, wondering if you are truly awake... or simply in yet another dream.

Somewhere between leaving Díaz's office and arriving at Harry's, that sense of the unexperienced yet familiar came upon me... and I knew I was going to say 'yes.' Walking the streets of San Francisco, I found myself looking again and again at the sky... wondering how soon the impossible things I'd seen there in my dreams would also arrive.

If Díaz was telling the truth, they were on their way.

"So, what's the occasion?" Harry asked, as he sat my drink on the bar. Harry is a big guy, Polynesian, with a taste for Hawai'ian shirts and good rum. He had dark hair beginning to go gray, pulled back into a ponytail, and authentic-looking South Pacific tattoos I knew damned well he'd gotten right here in the Mission.

"I just got offered a new job by the people I've been working for. I'm trying to figure out if I should take it."

"Jobs are good; this one seems to be doin' ya pretty well, Solly. What's to figure?"

"It's a really long-term commitment. If I do this, this is pretty much what I'm doing the rest of my life."

"You say that like it's a bad thing," Harry said. "I was willing to do the same thing both times I got married."

"It's still a big commitment."

It was real. All of it was real. I knew where the dreams came from at last; I knew what they came from. It was terrifying... but it was also an enormous relief. Whatever else I was, at least I wasn't crazy.

"So what's the rub?" I'd known Harry a long time. He'd been willing to run me a tab when no one else would, been there for me in other ways as well. As much as anyone, he deserved a straight answer—or at least as straight as I could manage.

"The boss is a big shot who likes to play hard ball, and he's put the squeeze on me before—on the other hand, he's offering a seat at the table, and the offer's legit."

"What you got yourself into, Solly? Sounds like some mob action."

I laughed. "Not quite, but there are some similarities—particularly if I screw up."

Harry laughed back, poured me another drink. "It's a tough world, little brother—ain't none of us gettin' by on our own. If it's a legit offer, take it. If it ain't, tell the big man to go fuck himself. Life's short, either way."

seven: kayce

"The Yanquis are fools, Kayce."

"I think their last election proves that, sir. They never should've given Texas the vote."

"There is that as well," Díaz said. "This man they have made President knows nothing of Majestic; Hopefully, it will be kept that way. It is bad enough that he babbles nonsense about 'making great again' his insane country. But that is not the Yanqui fool to whom I refer."

"I didn't think so, sir."

For once, I at least did not have to worry about missing dinner with my wife. Esmerelda had announced her plans to work late in the studio, made it plain that I was free to eat from a street cart, eat takeout at my desk, or subsist on bar snacks. The call from Mathilde had actually been welcome. It was better than grading papers and feeling sorry for myself.

The great man had been as good as his word. Against a backdrop of escalating 'mystery disk' reports, my role at BSI had changed yet again, and so had Saul's—whose professional skills as a writer were being put to an interesting new usage as a cover for what he was really doing. When someone like Hiram Díaz decides you have an increased 'need to know,' it is not a compliment—or a favor or a privilege. It might be an opportunity... but you can pretty well assume you're going to wind up paying for it.

"They are fools and they are lying to us, Kayce. You have read the report, yes?"

The report in question, tossed in my lap, was BSI's analysis of the incomplete 'Mystery Disk detector' data that had been previously delivered by Colonels Blaine and Hodge, distributed the day before to an extremely restricted audience. "Not really my field, but yes. What is it you think they're lying about?"

Díaz snorted. "Everything. How do you know a Yanqui is not lying? Easy—their lips do not move. I think that they are violating the Majestic Accords they themselves drafted to obtain our help. And you were in the room when they gave themselves away."

"Again, admiral, this isn't really my field."

"The technology of this is virtually no one's field—at least no one human. And that is how I know they are lying. Do you recall the answer when I asked how this breakthrough had been tested?"

"Something about 'cycling the Device'?" I said.

"Just so. It took decades to determine that the Device's drive system was still intact, decades more to determine how to activate it—and now they flick it on and off like a light switch. Either they are fools, or they know more than they are sharing. Then there is this 'detector' of theirs."

"At least they have shared that."

"True—but what they have shared makes no sense. For one thing, no Yanqui should know how to build such a thing."

It was a generalization, but not unreasonable. Ideology hampers innovation, and for decades people of talent have made the same decision my grandpa made and left the United States. The admiral was right: Something like a 'gravimetric field variance detector' should have been far beyond what passed for science in the U.S.

"Could this have anything to do with the redactions in the source data?" I asked.

Disdain shifted to contempt. "Stone is grandstanding, Kayce. This happens every time his budget for spying on his own people comes up for review. But that does not mean you are wrong—although I am highly doubtful the information he's chosen to withhold will answer these questions. I want you to uncover the truth. Sr. Ellsberg is going to help you."

"Saul's a writer, and I'm a history teacher. Are you sure you have the right people, Admiral?"

"You are entirely too modest, Kayce. I have seen your service record. Even though you joined BSI as a researcher, I have every confidence in placing you in the field. As for Ellsberg, he is key to what I have in mind. His abilities are growing. If the Yanquis are concealing what I think... he will know."

"What do you want to do, Admiral?"

"In a week, I attend the next Majestic conference at Patterson Aerodrome. You and Ellsberg shall accompany me. Ostensibly, this is to make presentations on your work. Your actual assignment is to find out whatever you can about the true state of the Yanqui research into the Device."

"BSI is full of people better qualified for this than I am. I can't even lie convincingly to my wife."

"Perhaps not, but you are very, very smart, Kayce. It is not as though you are being asked to go undercover as something you are not or assassinate anyone. And you may find you have more aptitude for this than you think." The great man smiled his dazzling, perfect smile. "I know I did."

＊ ＊ ＊ ＊

"I hadn't realized the job included travel."

"The job includes whatever the admiral says it does, Saul—regardless whatever your new contract might say."

I had been feeling a bit 'overwhelmed' after my meeting with Díaz, invited Saul out for coffee. It had been a while since either one of us had time for a coffee break, It was a nice day. We'd gotten our drinks to go, found a bench near the statue of Grand Admiral Castro.

"I'll be sure to act surprised when I get the call," Saul said.

"Please do."

There was a long silence as we sipped coffee and looked out across the bay, finally broken by Saul. "You know he told me everything, right?"

"The admiral doesn't tell anyone 'everything,'" I said. "But I do know that your security clearance just hit 'gold-alpha,' same as me, and you are now cleared to see the same material in your file I'm cleared to see. You should feel honored, by the way: Civilian contractors hardly ever get past 'bronze.' How does it feel?"

Saul chuckled. "Honestly, I have no idea how I feel. Being crazy was better than I thought it was. Any chance Dr. Abenard could just undo it and put me back?"

"You know more about it than I do... but I don't think it works that way."

"No," he chuckled again. "No, it does not. He thinks I'm a weapon, doesn't he?"

"Are you?"

"Maybe."

I hadn't been entirely truthful when I gave Saul a copy of Pop's first Sci-Rom. Pops only vaguely remembered having been stuck on a panel with a writer named 'Saul Ellsberg.'

But even if he'd remembered him perfectly, he wouldn't know him now.

The frightened, haunted, man Díaz had once sent me to arrest had lost weight, lost a lot of fear, gained something that almost looked like confidence. He was still haunted, but after the things Helene Abenard had told me, I could understand why.

He had changed, he was changing still. Where and how the process might end was no more something I could say or imagine than I could say whether or not Díaz had expected this outcome. I didn't humor myself that I was much more than a knight or a rook on the great man's human chessboard. I didn't expect I would see the full strategy much before checkmate.

But, given what sat on the other side of the board... that suited me just fine.

"So—what exactly is this conference, anyway?" Saul asked.

"I don't know much more than you," I told him. "From what the admiral tells me, not that different from any other small-focus scientific or academic conference—except for the fact that you could wind up in prison for the rest of your life just for confirming that it even exists."

Saul chuckled, sadly. "At this point, I could probably wind up in San Quentin just for confirming my own existence. Is there anything else you can tell me?"

"Just that it happens every year and the Estaditos always host it at Patterson Aerodrome, under the cover of a public aeronautics convention that conveniently happens at the same time."

"Sounds like an expensive cover. Is there really a good reason for all this?"

I laughed. "The Estaditos think so. According to the admiral, at least half of this is about the 'yanquis' reminding us who has possession of the Device. The aeronautics convention is a real convention."

"I think I've heard of it. There are U.S. Sci-Rom fans who go just to look at the new toys."

"That wouldn't surprise me. That's about as close as most Estaditos are likely to get to anything like a rocket plane or an aerostat."

"Or an 'aethership,'" Saul said.

"Or that."

eight: murphy

I'd found a thrift store near my hotel, made a modest investment in my wardrobe. I felt a lot more presentable in a pearl-snapped white shirt and a dark plaid blazer, even though I was still wearing dungarees and boots. "You still look like an 80s throwback," had been Case's sole comment.

Pythia smiled at me from her desk when I arrived at the library—apparently dressed as well for our 'date' in a long skirt and off-the-shoulder white blouse. I could still not honestly say if I was attracted to her or identify the impulse that had caused me to ask her out. But it was nice to again spend time with an actual human being who wasn't trying to kill me. It had been a while.

There had been less local history than I'd hoped in the Albuquerque public library, hardly anything about "ghost airships." But I was able to verify that a fairly important event in my world had happened here as well, with much the same official response—although orchestrating a cover-up that required coordination between at least three sovereign

'American' governments must've been a shit ton of fun for the local equivalents to what I used to be.

But I hadn't really come here to read up on unidentified aerial phenomena—there was plenty of that these days in the papers. What Pythia's library lacked in esoterica it more than made up for with a substantial Spanish language collection that I found useful for both primary and secondary mission research. I still didn't know what I was going to do when I finally confronted whatever lay behind that blinking light in my head... but I had an increasingly clear idea of how I was going to get there.

I'd seen even more workers decorating the plaza as I'd made my way to the library. The fiesta Pythia had invited me to was beginning to look promising. I tried to remember the last time I'd done anything comparable, was shocked to realize that I could remember nothing of the sort since Caroline had left me so many years ago. I had been dying for a long time before The Fortuned and The Obligate had seen fit to resurrect me. Longer than I had realized.

* * * *

"Should you like your fortune told, Miguel?"

"Oh, why not?" The street fair was in full swing, dozens of paper lanterns festooning trees all about the plaza, mariachi holding forth soulfully from a bandstand that had been raised in front of the church. We'd bought raspados from a street vendor as soon as we'd left the library and strolled the plaza. Now that the last delicious frozen bits were melting in the bottom of the paper cones, it was time to find some other amusement. There was a beer garden at one end of the plaza that looked promising... but Pythia did not drink. Crowds of people had arrived from other nearby towns and the nearby countryside. So as well had a number of vendors arrived to sell things to them.

The fortune teller had one of the most impressive booths of any of those who had set up shop in the plaza, a tent decorated with the usual assortment of occult images, fronted with a banner proclaiming the occupant to be 'Madame Isadora.' I had already started a new batch of fairy gold for the next leg of my journey. I could spare a few coins for a fortune I knew better than to expect anyone to foretell.

Pythia had bound her dark hair to one side, hanging over a shoulder bared by her blouse. She looked both younger and happier than the woman I had met a scant day before. Was she significantly 'older' than the hard-faced young stranger I saw in my mirror? Not really.

A few yards away, the ghost of Colvin Case was smiling as well, oblivious to the fact that fiesta attendees were walking through him. I had relented and left the social interface on, having gotten a promise of good behavior and reserving the right to switch it off as I saw fit.

"One?" Madame Isadora asked. "Or both?"

"Both," I said, dispensing the appropriate coins. "Ladies first," I said, bowing slightly to Pythia.

The interior of the tent was dark and a little stuffy. Madame Isadora wore a gown and headdress that might well have come from the same bolt of garish fabric her tent had been made from, sat at a small table covered with the same stuff, holding the usual accoutrements of her trade and a couple of candles. She was dark-complected, with iron-gray hair.

Pythia sat across from her. "Your hand, please," Madame Isadora said.

After studying Pythia's palm for a few moments, Madame Isadora consulted the cards as well, then spoke. "I see past pain and disappointments, decisions you've lived to regret. Something has just entered your life that you do not understand, but you find... very attractive. I see long life and eventual happiness." She looked up from the cards and into Pythia's eyes. Her own eyes were very dark. "I see also a question in your mind—do you want it answered?"

"Yes, please."

"The answer is 'no'—at least not in the way you think. But there is no harm in any of what you have done."

Pythia blushed, and the sadness I had seen before returned. "I understand. Thank you." She stood, then smiled again when she looked at me. "It is your turn, Miguel."

I took the seat at the table and offered up my own hand. Madame Isadora looked it, pausing theatrically while running through her memorized list of vague bromides.

Then she looked again.

Then she looked up at Pythia, "He is... not easy to read. Could you perhaps wait outside?"

I looked at Pythia, who nodded and stepped out of the tent. I turned back to Madame Isadora, who had produced a small box from a cupboard at her feet. "For you, I need the... other cards."

Clearing away her other implements, she laid a row of cards face down. "Aren't you going to ask me to concentrate or something?" I said.

"No," she replied.

She turned over the first card. "This," she said, "Is how you came into this world." The image on the card showed a shooting star descending from a starry night sky, a storm-tossed ocean behind it.

She turned over the next card. It showed a road in a forest. Upon the road, a broken chariot. "This is how you found your way forward."

Then the next. Beneath a blazing sun, a man in a black kilt stood with a great black sword stood over two vanquished foes. "This is how you were tested."

And the next. A garden bower. In it, a woman smiling sweetly and sadly, her hair and gown both long and dark. "This is how you are tempted."

Then, the last card. A pyramid temple grew up from a jungle. On its summit, two figures... too small to be seen. "And this your destiny. You know what this is... don't you?"

I nodded.

Madame Isadora gathered up the cards, returned them to their case. "I have something for you," she said.

Returning to her cupboard, she removed another object and placed it on the table. "This places you under their protection," she said. The object before me was a curved dagger, seemingly of silver, carved with symbols different from the ones on her tent.

Symbols I knew. "Whose protection?" I asked, my voice suddenly grown hoarse.

"Las hermanas," she whispered. "This moon dagger will take you to them, oh man of another world. And to your destiny."

"Did I not know better, I might think you were cheating on me," Esmerelda sulked.

"With who, Hiram Díaz? I'm even more immune to his charms than your mother—for what I hope are obvious reasons."

"What of this 'research assistant' of yours?"

"He would be flattered by your jealousy and as confused by it as I am," I told her. "Saul Ellsberg is almost as old as Pops. In other words, not my type—and very clear on the fact that I'm a happily married woman. And he's not my assistant. He got promoted."

"At least if it were to cheat on me, this trip of yours might make sense."

I was packing for an early departure. Esmerelda was trying to pick a fight. Luckily, I'm good at multitasking. "I've already told you more than I should. Anything I've left out, I've left out because I can't tell you everything—and you know I can't."

Esmerelda was sitting crosslegged at the foot of the bed drinking wine—not quite Two Peso Chuck, but not exactly the good stuff either. She poured me a glass. I took a sip, sat it on the nightstand. I had no intention of flying with a hangover. She was wearing a nightie I'd bought her some years before, when I was still on active duty.
If she meant to be a distraction, it was working.

"Hiram will not be content until you are as deep in intrigue as he is. You should have stayed at the Academy, Corazon—it is more honest."

She had a point, and I had to wonder—why, exactly, had I ever accepted a BSI posting in the first place? It had been interesting enough, even before Admiral Díaz moved me to the 'Ghost Airship' desk, but I'd never been particularly impressed with the supposed glamor of intelligence work, never seen it as essential to the security of the republic, or in any other way saw what I was doing as superior to any other career option. But I love a good challenge... and nothing in my life had ever challenged me more.

"I'm sure I'll wind up back at the Academy soon enough, darling. And I can't think of a single reason why Admiral Díaz would want me as 'deep in intrigue' as he is... I'm not even sure it's possible." I zipped shut my duffel and hoisted it. A little heavy, maybe, but I'm on the small side; the combined weight should be well within allowance. I dropped it in the hallway where it would be easily found in the morning, not in the way in the meanwhile.

I returned to bed, sliding out of my skivvies and under the covers. A little wine would be fine, just not a lot. "So do you just want to sit there and sulk? Or would you like to show your wife a decent sendoff?"

* * * *

My orders had called for me to be at the Naval Preserve Aerodrome for a 0600 departure. I had reserved a cab for 0400, both to ensure timely arrival and diminish the odds of a last-minute argument with my wife. The plan worked. Esmerelda was snoring gently when my watch alarm vibrated me into consciousness, and continued to as I slipped out of bed and into a flight suit. Since I was supercargo, not crew, I could as easily have opted for standard uniform. But I knew from experience that I could quickly and quietly don a flight suit in the dark.

The cab showed up as scheduled; not long after, I was on the Naval Preserve Aerodrome tarmac, making my way to the airship moorings. It was easy enough to find RCAS Morrison. Nothing else on the field was staged for departure. I just followed the spotlights.

The Morrison was a trimaran, a blunt arrowhead shape made up of three-hectometre aerostat hulls connected by two cargo decks, outrigged by a half dozen variable geometry turbo impellers, three to a side, on stubby 'wings.' It was rigged to the tarmac for loading—four short moorings front and aft, loading conveyors extended into the cargo decks. As I drew closer, I could see the ground crew and ship's complement in the early light, other figures as well.

Unsurprisingly, one of them was Hiram Díaz.

Like myself, the admiral was wearing flight suit and cap, a duffel bag on the tarmac next to his feet. He was speaking to another man, similarly attired with the addition of a leather jacket. As I came closer, the admiral favored me with one of his brilliant smiles. "Hola, Kayce, and good morning. Captain Howard, permit me to introduce Commander Cullen—who shall be flying with us today."

Captain Howard was a compact man, scarcely taller than myself. Air Navy tends short for the same reason as the submarine service—in both cases, compartment space tends to be limited. Additionally, Air Navy has to account for every single kilo being taken aloft. Very rarely do either officers or crew include anyone as large as Hiram Díaz.

"Welcome aboard, Commander," Howard said with an offhanded salute. "You're very welcome to join us on the flight deck for departure, as long as you can stay out of the way—which I expect you can." He gestured to a nearby junior officer. "Mr. Phillips," he said. "Help the commander stow her gear." He turned back to me. "I doubled up Phillips and some of the other middies, wound up with a cabin you can share with Sr. Ellsberg. I hope that's not a problem."

"Not at all, sir—just don't tell my wife."

ten: ellsberg

Harry Kamealoha was welcome to try to tell Admiral Díaz to fuck himself if he liked. They were both big guys, and I had seen Harry singlehandedly clear his bar of sailors who didn't know it was time to go—but Harry had never met a 'sailor' quite like Hiram Díaz.

So, yeah: I signed the new contract. The new job title was 'Research and Media Analyst' and a pay raise went with it. But the job duties remained 'TBD.'

"Please understand," Díaz had told me. "This is a cover, even though the work you are doing is real and serves a real purpose. Your real work will never be detailed in any document accessible to anyone who does not have security clearance at the highest level.

"You now report to me, not Commander Cullen. On my authority, you now have security clearances equal to hers—but please do not assume her 'need to know' and yours are automatically the same."

"How do I know what I should and should not talk about?" I asked him.

"Best that you assume not. It would be a good habit to get into."

* * * *

With the new title came other changes as well.

I got a new office, for one thing. I needed it. I now had research assistants of my own.

Lieutenants Schuyler and Greenberg were as bright and shiny as new pesos—and not much older. Their enthusiasm for being assigned to 'Project Phantasos' reminded me just how old I really was.

Worse yet, they knew who I was.

"I can't tell you what an honor this is," Lieutenant Schuyler gushed. "I love your books."

We were sitting in the same conference room I'd once been led into by a pair of RCN Marines. At the head of the table was Hiram Díaz, dressed as usual like a deckhand. Kayce was there as well, trying not to look amused, as well as Mathilde Juarez—who wasn't even trying.

"Sr. Ellsberg does us all a great favor," Díaz said. Any amusement he felt was completely contained. "You will learn much from him, I am sure."

I'd heard the rumors for years, long before Mystery Disks Revealed turned up in my mailbox or mystery disks revealed themselves in my dreams. Among people who cared about such things, it was not so much a question of if there was a conspiracy—just a question of how much was being covered up. And Sci-Rom was full of people who cared very much about such things.

And, apparently, also full of people who worked for BSI.

"The first story was of modest concern," Díaz had said, they day I signed the contract. "Ignorant Texicans had already made it public; we had already discredited it. But it brought you to our attention. Your second story touched on matters we had only recently become aware of—which is why it had to be suppressed."

I couldn't complain too much. 'Armada of Ghosts' might've been the most ambitious thing I'd ever written, but at the end of the day it was the same thing I'd been doing for the better part of two decades: recycling the dreams that had made my life miserable, selling them on the cheap as bad fiction.

Getting suppressed and blacklisted by Bureau of Strategic Intelligence, on the other hand, had turned into the best thing that had ever happened to me.

Project Phantasos was a unique opportunity for a Sci-Rom writer—even though it involved writing fiction of a slightly different sort.

"The Estaditos have been doing this for years," Díaz explained. "Given that their media is essentially state run by the people who own their government, it is easy for them to suppress and discredit things they do not wish known. California is a republic; its citizens have protected rights—which means we must be more creative."

By the end of the meeting, guidelines for that 'creativity' had been established and my new staff returned to my new office suite with a week's worth of writing assignments. Mathilde and Kayce left as well, but Díaz asked that I stay.

"I have asked Dr. Abenard to make time for a session with you this afternoon," the admiral said. "This will be different from your previous sessions. Upon awakening, you will remember everything."

"Why is this happening, Admiral?"

"It is happening because it must. Too many things are occurring and I have too few answers. I suspect as well I am being lied to by allies, allies I had thought at least conditionally worthy of trust. You had once asked me if 'it was real.' I could not answer. Now I must. It is all real, Saul Ellsberg—even the parts you had hoped were lies."

"Twice in a month," Harry said. "This mean you're a regular again?"

"Too soon to say," I told him. "We'll find out when I get back in town."

"This part of your new job?"

"Yes and no. It's... complicated."

I had been to the U.S. before on a book tour; hadn't liked it. The cities were all overcrowded and dirty. Even at book signings, the amount of casual racism was staggering. I was questioned more about being Jewish on the tour than I had been in my entire previous life.

But Kayce was right: my job description included whatever Hiram Díaz said it included... and that now meant a return visit to the United States.

Among other things.

"There are things at Patterson Aerodrome you will find... familiar," the admiral had told me. "I will need to know of these things."

This is how it works when you dream of impossible things and things that come true. There comes a day when the distinction between dream and reality effectively ends, and existence becomes a continued waking dream, or perhaps a nightmare... and you can no longer tell if you are causing the dreams or if the dreams are causing you.

"Now you know," Helene Abenard had said upon waking me... with a look of sadness and compassion beyond anything I had ever seen before.

I could contain it—she'd also shown me that—there was now a switch in my mind. I didn't have to be asleep to see impossible things. I could also truly sleep for perhaps the first time in my life.

But it came at a cost.

I'd stopped off at Harry's for pretty much the same reason I had the last time. I was trying to wrap my mind around what my life was becoming and finding it not so easy. Definitely, I needed a drink. But more than that, I needed the familiarity of my old and smaller life... at least for a little while.

"Try to act surprised," Kayce had said—as though what she was telling me was in any way surprising in the first place. But she couldn't know that, and neither could Díaz. There was no need for them to know.

I wished I didn't.

This is how it works when you have dreams that come true: suddenly something you're doing or experiencing seems familiar, sometimes to the point of even knowing what someone is going to say before they say it. Then you try to remember why. Then you remember that you dreamed it.

I had known before the words left his mouth that Hiram Díaz intended me to go with him to Wright-Patterson—no, that's not right—just 'Patterson,' here. I knew what he expected to find when we got there.

I also knew how he expected to get there, and that scared me more than anything—even though I couldn't tell anyone why.

* * * *

The morning of the day it was supposed to happen came all too soon. I'd given my bright and shiny lieutenants a week's worth of disinformation to write, instructions to talk to Mathilde if they ran out of things to do. On Kayce's advice, I'd hired a cab to get to the Aerodrome. "I know you like riding the train," she'd said. "But you really need to make sure you get there on time."

When I'd been trying to figure out how to write my own version of Clarke Kimball's 'aetherships,' I'd read up on both airships and submarines, figuring that anything that flew through space would be a lot like both. Even though I'd never actually been on an airship, I at least sort of knew what to expect. I also knew that a lot of people were afraid to fly—just not the way I was afraid.

My RCN badge got the cab a temporary permit that got all the way to the airship moorings. After that, I knew where I was going. 444

California Air Navy flies ships in many sizes and shapes. I knew the one I was looking for was a big triangle that reminded me a lot of something else I'd once seen. It wasn't hard to find. It was lit up for departure and surrounded by people... including the ones I knew.

Kayce and Díaz were both wearing flight suits, talking to another man dressed the same. Helene Abenard and I were probably going to be the only people onboard wearing anything else. She was there as well. Her dark eyes were hidden behind very large and even darker sunglasses, her dark hair concealed behind a grey scarf.

This too reminded me of something... but I could not think what.

"Hola, Saul," Kayce said as I joined them, "And good morning—why so pale? You don't get airsick, do you?"

"Not as far as I know," I said.

"It's not strictly regulation," the captain said when Díaz introduced me, "but you and Dr. Abenard have pretty good credentials for civilians. You are welcome to join the admiral and Commander Cullen as observers for takeoff. It's a pretty boring trip for the most part—hell, the ship pretty much flies itself—but we'll be passing over the Sierra Nevada range not long after we raise ship... this time of day it should be quite the sight to see."

"Thanks," I told him.

* * * *

This is how it works when you have dreams that come true: suddenly something you're doing or experiencing seems familiar, sometimes to the point of even knowing what someone is going to say before they say it. Then you try to remember why. Then you remember that you dreamed it.

By the time I joined Kayce and Díaz in the back of the Morrison's flight deck, the feeling of inescapable familiarity had become overpowering. Looking forward, I saw the pilot and copilot at the front of the deck, before them the broad windscreen and an array of data displays. I knew these things because I'd read about them. But I knew them anyway. Behind them sat the captain, to his left and right the flight engineer and the communications officer. Behind them, observers—us.

Díaz had taken the seat immediately behind the flight engineer, with Helene to his side and Kayce behind him.
I took the last observer seat next to Kayce. Behind me, a ladder led upward into the rest of the ship. Behind and below it, the gangway we'd used to board. As we seated, the gangway folded up into the back of the compartment

with a soft sigh of hydraulics. We would soon be underway.

As the sun began to glint over the hills, a flare went up in the sky. I knew it meant we were cleared to take off.

Then the engines roared to life, holding the airship at station over the tarmac with vertical reverse thrust while the mooring lines were cast loose and reeled in. From where we sat, we could see it all. Then the captain told the pilot "Take her up". The impellers pivoted and the ground fell away. Even though I had never flown before, it was all very, very familiar.

Helene looked back at me. Despite the enormous sunglasses, I could see the concern. "You're distraught, Saul—what is it? What have you seen?"

"It's nothing," I told her. Nothing anyone can do anything about. "Everything will be fine."

* * * *

It wasn't until we were over foothills, approaching mountains that the thing happened.

"Captain," said the copilot, "I have numerous unidentified radio detect targets closing fast from due north."

"Could you be more specific, Mr. Everett? What do you mean by 'numerous' and 'fast'?"

Before Lieutenant Everett could reply, he didn't have to.

Morrison's flight deck was hung from the centerfront of the center aerostat. From the broad airscreen windows, we could see everything not hidden by the hull above us. Televisor screens above the windows showed everything else.

We were surrounded by an array of glowing red lights—a dodecahedron, I somehow knew—holding perfect station around us.

"This better not be something of yours, Admiral," Howard called back from his command seat. Ashen-faced, Díaz shook his head.

"Foo Fighters," I whispered.

"What did you say?" asked Kayce.

"Never mind," I said. "They haven't happened here yet."

Helene turned and looked at me. "If there's something you know, Saul, we all need to know it."

Then, as one, the red lights turned blue and flashed brighter than the sun. As the light faded, so did everything else... including the sound of the engines.

"You know something, Saul," Helene said. "What does this mean? What happened?"

"Anyone on this deck who is not a member of this crew needs to hold their peace," roared Howard. "No offense, admiral—but that includes you!"

I knew no one else would say anything. I also knew it didn't matter. "This entire ship just lost power, Helene. Engines, flight control—everything. We're floating free into a range of mountains."

The admiral surprised me. "It means," he said in a low voice, "that unless Captain Howard and his crew can restore navigational control and power... we are very likely all dead."

eleven: murphy

I could've taken other and possibly shorter routes to get to the blinking light in my implants' heads-up display. But I'd been given no exact timeline to complete my solo mission in a foreign universe—and even though it looked like that mission might be getting more critical in some ways, anyone who might object to how I was conducting it was far, far away.

Fuck them in any case. I was going to go home—or at least as close as I was ever likely to get. I was now in what would be considered 'Texas' on either side of the wormhole—the Hill Country, basically, referred to locally as 'Balcones Province, Republic of Texas.' Some of the hills in question almost qualified as small mountains. I was on one of them.

I'd parked the Armstrong by the side of the road for a brief break and a chance to enjoy the scenery. There was, after all, a reasonable chance I would never pass this way again... at least not in this world. To the south, I saw sagebrush covered hills, some carpeted as well with wildflowers. In the world I'd left behind, this was more or less a suburb of Austin and the hills were covered with McMansions, not sage. I preferred this version.

Further southeast, at the edge of my enhanced vision, the hills grew greener and lower and would eventually become the coastal plains that led to the Gulf of Mexico. There, I would find myself in the only real city in all of Texas. There I also would find the first of several highways that would take me further south and into Central America. How close the Armstrong could get me to that blinking light in my head was almost as open to question as what I'd find when I got there. But I was confident in the old bike. As long as I could find fuel and something reasonably close to a road, the Armstrong would do what it was made for... and so would I.

There remained as well the question of just how much the data ghost painting that blinking target could really be trusted, but it wasn't like I had a huge number of options. Case Prime had been as much a double agent as myself, albeit under different circumstances. But I had reasons of my own to believe his 'ghost'—reasons of which he knew nothing, that I'd taken some small pains to keep to myself.

The fact that whatever Case was targeting had remained static since I'd arrived in this world made it seem highly unlikely that the 'angel' we were hunting would turn out to be an analog of my old friend Morningstar. The stranded immortal who had amused himself by alternately masquerading as human and as Satan had wandered my world like the damned soul he truly was. It was just as likely that we were tracking what Morningstar had called a 'Seraphim Stone'—a nonsentient piece of the same stuff from which 'god' had made 'angels.' Then again, it was just as likely that he'd gotten bored with wandering and settled into a single place, or perhaps had gone mad or catatonic. I wouldn't know until I got there.

And I still had no idea what I was going to do when I did.

It was a pretty view, but I had work to do. I got back on the Armstrong and gunned the engine to life. The delays I'd encountered in Albuquerque had been useful, even revealing—but they were still delays. I had some catching up to do.

* * * *

Pythia was waiting when I left the fortuneteller tent, smiling an uncertain smile. "That was strange," she said.

"More than you know." It had taken a little work, but I had managed to fit the moon dagger into a boot scabbard that currently didn't have anything else tucked into it. It was either that, or the waistband of my dungarees... which didn't seem like a really great idea. "So what would you like to do now?"

"Festivals are fun," she said. "But they are also quite loud. Talking to you is nice. I know a park not far from here where the view of the city is lovely and where we can talk—and I do not mind riding there on your motorcycle."

* * * *

I'd given her a choice of the sidecar or riding pillion. To my surprise, she had taken the latter, her head against my shoulder as she gave me directions to a park where we could talk... or whatever else it might please her to do.

The park was as pleasant as advertised, at the summit of a nearby hill. Below us were the lights of the mission town this world's Albuquerque had largely remained. Above us, stars and a moon brilliant in the clear desert sky. In the distance, I could still hear the mariachis playing in the plaza.

Parking the Armstrong, we found a bench beneath a weathered oak. Pythia tucked her feet beneath her as she sat, seeming more birdlike than ever. She took my arm, laying her head against my shoulder. "This is nice," she said.

"I agree."

"What did Madame Isadora tell you, Miguel?"

"Oh, the usual: Long life, fortune, love."

"You are lying, precocious boy—for there is nothing 'usual' about you. But if it is not something you wish to speak of, I understand."

"I'm hardly a 'boy,' Pythia."

"You are not, though you seem as one. You should kiss me, I think... that I might know for sure."

So I did.

"No," she said after a bit. "Not a boy... most certainly a man, and a very strange one. Kiss me again, Miguel."

As I took her into my arms, she suddenly stiffened and gasped, staring past my shoulder. "What is that?"

I broke the embrace, turned to see what she had seen.

Drifting over Albuquerque was an object that seemed all too familiar, right down to the ornate tracings in what looked like metal. I was not incredibly surprised when a beam of light speared down—either upon or close to the hotel where I was staying. Apparently not finding what it sought, the beam winked out as the object continued silently southward.

"That," I said, "is what I believe the newspapers call a 'ghost airship.'"

"What is it doing, Miguel?"

"Looking for something, I think."

"And how can you know this?" she asked.

"Because I am the thing it looks for."

* * * *

The next day, I left Albuquerque. I hadn't found the answers I'd been looking for, but the ones I'd found were perhaps as good.

In any event, they'd have to do.

I was many miles further down the highway before I thought to stop again.

I had left 'social interface' activated at the festival, switched it off when Pythia suggested hopping onto the Armstrong and making way to a quieter locale, left it switched off for a long time afterward.

Basically, I needed to think.

Either I or what I carried was being sought, by an agency no more of this world than myself. I both do and do not believe in coincidences. One school in which I had been trained saw them as surface elements of deeper causation. Another school believed in no deeper causation than itself. Whether anything like either of those schools existed in this world remained to be seen, but I was beginning to have my suspicions. If what I suspected was true, my mission here had become more urgent. But it also seemed likely that I might have both adversaries and allies I had not looked for. I would have to proceed very carefully.

As I proceeded southward, I was increasingly struck by the beauty of the places I traveled through. I had started out in a Pacific Northwest strikingly similar to the one where I had spent decades before my rebirth—just as lovely, just as green, just as much the 'Cascadia' where I had once sought refuge from a world that had grown too complex and too dangerous, in which I no longer felt at home.

But now I was in another version of that world. And it had none of those things.

All the library research in the world could not tell me what my ordinary human senses told me now. The air I drew into my lungs was clean. There was a crisp chill in the night air that an unfolding global climate catastrophe had taken from the 'Texas' of my birth many, many years ago.

The Fortuned wanted to know what had diverged this Earth from the one where they'd recruited me. It might well have been as simple as the absence of their own corrupting influence and others like them. Humanity had made bad choices here as well, but not as many. Perhaps centuries remained before this world faced the hard choices my own world had forced itself into; perhaps those choices might be avoided altogether.

By the time I made it to the rolling hills of central Texas, I had reached a decision of sorts. I would keep faith with those who had recreated me and sent me here, but I would also keep faith with what I still thought of, more than not, as my own kind. It wouldn't be easy—but if I had wanted 'easy,' I could've just gone ahead and died.

Finally, I found myself at the very edge of the hill country, where it gave way to the coastal plains that would eventually become the beaches rimming the Gulf of Mexico. The day was failing, and clouds were piling up in the sky in what I knew would become thunderstorms and torrential rain. My enhanced senses found what appeared to be a cave in the side of a hill overlooking the highway I traveled. I decided I would make camp there for the night.

The cave wasn't big enough for both the Armstrong and me, but there was enough of a clearing that I could lay the old bike against the hillside and cover it with the tarp I'd acquired on my way out of Oregon. The cave stank slightly of an animal's lair, but it was an old scent. My principal concern had been rattlesnakes, but I found none—truth be told, in my present condition, I was perhaps as much a danger to them as they to me. Certainly, I could now strike as quickly.

I had been putting off another consultation with Case, but I didn't have the luxury of putting it off much longer. To the immediate south of my present location was another sleepy former mission town like Albuquerque, this one the site of a famous battle that here had turned out somewhat differently. It would be nice to visit this world's San Antonio, but on some other occasion. To the east was the sprawling metropolis of 'Greater Galveston,' the last major city on this continent before I turned south toward the blinking red point where I would, one way or another, complete my mission… and discharge at least some small part of the Obligation I'd accepted.

I'd said farewell to Pythia Cortes before leaving Albuquerque, even though the thought of simply leaving had crossed my mind as well. The town was all abuzz with talk of the spectral object that had appeared in the midst of the fiesta the night before. If my suspicions were correct, 'federales' of some sort or other would soon be arriving to investigate—who might also be asking if any strangers had recently arrived fitting a particular description. Best for me that any such stranger be departed before they arrive.

She had blushed slightly when I walked into the library. She was dressed as demurely as she had been when I met her. In preparation for my journey, I was once again wearing a battered leather jacket over a white singlet and dungarees, goggles hanging around my neck. I probably looked like one of the extras from The Wild Ones—not that anyone would know that here.

"I can spare a moment," she said, joining me at the door. "No more."

We stepped outside together. I found her embracing me suddenly—and just as suddenly pulling away. "I know you are leaving," she said, smiling sadly. "And I know it is best."

"It is," I told her. "But perhaps not for the reasons you think." I had been wondering what and how much to say to her after the night before. What could I say, when there was so little I could say of myself?

But there was one thing I needed to say.

"I want you to know," I said, "that I find you utterly enchanting—and likely would've done, even were I not enchanted." I traced a pattern in the air before us. I hadn't been sure it would work, but it did—the sigil glowed briefly, barely visible in the full light of day, then faded. From her quick intake of breath, I knew she'd seen it as well.

"Oh! I beg forgiveness—I did not know!" Again, she blushed... even more this time.

"Blessed be, little sister," I told her. "As Madame Isadora said when she answered your question... 'no harm done.' And I hope none done to you."

She smiled her sad smile. "Less than did you stay, my brother in the Craft. Blessed be to you as well."

We then kissed again, and I felt her eyes upon my back as I cinched my goggles into place and mounted the Armstrong. I did not look back... for there was no need. And many miles to go before rest would be mine.

* * * *

"You know, bro—just switching me off like that is kinda rude."

"Leaving you on would've been even ruder—at least you got to enjoy the festival, right?"

"About as much as I get to 'enjoy' anything." I had decided I'd put it off as long as I could. I knew the data ghost was going to be cranky, but he'd managed to make himself essential to my mission. And as long as it didn't involve fashion sense or women, his advice continued to be useful.

Case was still in 'cowboy' mode, but he had toned it down considerably from his last manifestation. He had manifested an image across me on the other side of the campfire I'd built at the mouth of the cave where I planned to spend the night.

I was beginning to notice minor imperfections in the illusion of himself he was uploading into my visual implants. He had the effect down of being illuminated by firelight, but the flashes of lightning in the distance didn't 'reflect' on him at all. I thought about saying something, decided not to. Even though the chips in my head he lived in had a lot of capacity, I preferred to not think how much of that capacity was being used to humor the vanity of a sentient computer virus.

He was still sulking. "Thanks to your need for private sexy time with that little librarian, I didn't get to see your last 'ghost airship' encounter, you know—too bad you didn't think to record it... but I guess you had other things on your mind, old buddy."

"If I didn't know better, I'd say you were jealous, Case."

"You're goddam right I'm jealous," he grumbled. "Look, I don't give one faint fuck what you do with your dick—we're just friends, okay? Am I jealous that you have one? Bloody right."

"If I can ever figure out a way to do something about that, I promise it is at the top of my list," I told him. "If we complete this mission and return, maybe The Obligate can download you into some hardware of your own, instead of just hitting me with a shit ton of antivirus software—particularly after I tell them how much help you were. And, for the record, my dick isn't getting nearly as much action as you think it is—not that it's any of your fucking business."

Once again, I heard a ghostly dry chuckle in my head. "I'm pretty sure you'd put in a good word for me if you ask for recall at the end of all this—are you?"

"Am I what?"

"Planning to go back. Seems to me, you kinda like it here."

He had a point. Even though we were all cavemen compared to The Fortuned, my own Earth would look like what was locally called 'Sci-Rom' if any of the locals ever saw it. With a few exceptions, every single technology was more advanced in my timeline. But my Earth was also drowning in the collective waste of what would soon be over 8 billion people and counting, was more probably than not gearing up for yet another of the world wars that had never happened here—only this time, it really would be the 'war to end all wars'... and likely the end of humanity as well.

Another option, if I were to believe all that I had been told, might be to remain among The Fortuned and The Obligate. Evangeia had made it plain that I would be welcomed, even though I did not even share her status as a half-breed—or perhaps I did; whatever they had done to me on my Earth's moon was continuing to change me, in ways small and large.

But even if The Fortuned felt a need to maintain their agents in every single Earth their science uncovered, did I really have a need to be one of those agents? I had been told that the life I'd been given was mine, once my mission was complete. The option of remaining here had been held out all along.

"The jury's still out on that," I eventually said. "And it will be until I've done what I was sent here to do. Whatever decision I make, we'll talk. You've pretty much made sure of that by hacking your way into my targeting system. But we'll talk, anyway. I'm going to need all the help I can get to finish this thing."

"Not that I have a lot of choice, but I trust you. Thanks, old buddy."

"De nada."

"Meanwhile," he said, "there's something I need to ask you about."

"As long as it doesn't involve my sex life, ask away." By now, it was beginning to rain and the flashes of lightning Case didn't respond to were becoming more frequent. Case's avatar 'stood up' and walked around the edge of the clearing in front of the cave—an almost perfect illusion of a man stretching his legs after having sat too long on the ground.

"That last night in Albuquerque," he said, "at the fiesta. Your little librarian girlfriend talked you into getting your fortune told. What did you see?"

"What do you mean, 'what did I see'? You were there?"

He laughed. "Whether or not I go to the trouble of painting a picture in your implants, of course I'm 'there' if you have social switched on. The cards, old buddy—what did you see on the cards?"

"Maybe a better question, since you bring it up, is what you saw—you go first." Madame Isadora had sent Pythia from the tent for a reason. Maybe a reason I shared.

The ghost chuckled. "Fine. Be that way. Okay, I saw the old lady in the gypsy outfit lay out what I'm guessing were supposed to be something like tarot cards. She looked at them, you looked at them, you both acted like there was something there—but as far as I'm concerned, those cards were as blank and white as a fresh sheet of paper."

Now the lightning was coming even more frequently and accompanied by peals of thunder that were getting louder as well. I hadn't been in a Texas thunderstorm in a long time, but I was about to be smack in the middle of one. The raindrops were now getting fat and heavy, but Case's avatar was no more affected by them than by lightning or thunder.

"Your turn," he said. "What did you see?"

This wasn't going to be easy. I couldn't exactly alienate the ghost in my head, but there were other people and things I had even less interest in alienating. Things and people Case probably didn't believe in... and probably couldn't see if he did.

But I had to try.

"Who do you think I really worked for, all those years, Colvin... back when we were both with The Company?"

The ghost laughed a nasty laugh. "They go by a lot of names. The ones that put me in a tank, the ones that turned you into a double agent, like to call themselves 'The Order'—at least that's what I recall you calling them."

"Correct," I said. "Here's another question, and then maybe I can answer yours. Did you really think there was nothing more to The Order than interdimensional ETs with advanced technology?"

The wind was beginning to rise as well, as the thunder grew into a sound like artillery strikes. There was a strange look in Case's eyes. The lightning now reflected from the illusion of his body. Even as the rain now struck the illusion of his face, the wind drove the illusion of his hair.

He laughed again, nastier still. "In case you forgot, old buddy, there's nothing more to me than 'interdimensional ETs with advanced technology.' If there's something else going on, lay it on me—cause I'd really like to know!"

The wind was now a banshee howl, pebbles of hail mixed with the rain. The lightning flashes so bright they left afterimages... or were they?

Sufficiently advanced technology is indistinguishable from magic. Unless you've ever seen the real thing.

I traced a sigil in the air—not quite the one I had made for Pythia, but close enough. It took the light of fire and lightning and bent it into a searing blue shape hanging in the darkness. It did not fade.

"Case, I do not know whether it is that you could not see what was on those cards or that you should not—but if you are blind to this sign, then I can say no more until I am sure."

More flashes of acid-bright lightning, more after images in their wake, only now I was sure... they were not afterimages.

Red, unblinking eyes surrounded me in the dark, eyes set into misshapen skulls atop oddly ambiguous bodies. Was that as well a flutter of... wings?

Whatever else Case had to say was lost to me. If the lightning had not struck us, it was so close as to not matter. The thunder roared on and on as my campfire was snuffed out like a match. For a moment, I could see nothing but endless massed shapes in the darkness, endless unblinking red and hungry eyes.

Then the thunder crashed again... and I saw nothing.

About the Author

A.J. Curry is a writer with interests including history, fantasy, science fiction, and the occult-in no particular order, and not excluding other interests as well. Their preferred beverage is a dirty martini with pepper-infused vodka.

About the Publisher

Rose City Digital is a Portland-based boutique digital agency offering a wide range of creative and technical consulting services. RCD Press is their publishing consultancy, providing services and assistance to Pacific Northwest self-published authors.

For more information, visit https://rosecity.digital.

Dawn Matter

Published 2025 by

RCD Press, Portland, OR

979-8-9985988-3-8

Paperback